QUEEN TAKES JAGUARS

A THEIR VAMPIRE QUEEN NOVELLA

JOELY SUE BURKHART

QUEEN TAKES JAGUARS

One vampire queen.
Four jaguar Blood sworn to protect her.
Now all she needs...
is the Aztec jaguar god to sire her heir.

Mayte has spent the last century increasing her power as queen of House Zaniyah by calling more Blood to her side. She loves her jaguar protectors, but even her alpha hasn't been able to give her a child. Without a daughter to continue the queendom, their line—and the Zaniyah power—will die out.

She needs a god to sire her daughter, and for a queen who calls jaguars as Blood... only one god will do. Tepeyollotl is rumored to sleep in mythical Aztlán. Desperate for a daughter, she sets out to find the legendary origin site of the mighty Aztec people.

Though she has no idea how she'll bend the formidable god to her will.

1

MAYTE

I only ever saw her in dreams.

If she told me her name, I never remembered it later. The dreams were so real. She smelled like night-blooming jasmine and vanilla, and her black hair was thick, heavy silk that hung down to her waist. Her eyes were a dark, endless blue like a midnight sky. And her power…

I had never felt a queen like her before, waking or asleep. In her presence, I forgot to breathe.

She had to be real. Even if I couldn't remember her name.

"I am real," she assured me, drifting through my sleepy mind like a ghostly haze. "However, I'll be leaving this life soon. My years are numbered."

My heart shattered. She was my mentor and friend, as sad as that might be, considering that I didn't even know who she was. We had talked endlessly through many nights. She had taught me so many things that helped me better understand my power, especially how to grow that power to protect my family.

House Zaniyah was small compared to the other Aima clans. We were secluded, exactly as we liked it. The powerful

Triune houses couldn't care less about our small Mexican nest, even though I was one of the few queens to be born in the past two hundred years. My mysterious friend had admitted that my birth was why she had sought me out. Young queens were few and far between, and even at my age, I was considered young. The only other queen younger than me had been the New York City queen's daughter.

Even here in Mexico, the rumors had still reached us from Keisha Skye's court, including the news of her daughter's death. Making me the last living queen born in recent centuries.

I don't know how much help I'd actually been to my dream friend. I had no idea who my father was, and my mother had died at my birth. If Grandmama knew, she had refused to tell me.

"Why are you dying?" I asked.

"A plan I set in motion before you were born comes to fruition soon. I will invest all my power and love into this spell, so that my daughter may live free, untouched by the political games so rampant in our courts."

My throat ached. Was that why my mother had died? To have me?

I wanted a daughter more than anything to carry on our Zaniyah power, but if I had to die… I had so much to do yet. I couldn't leave an infant daughter unprotected.

Like Mama had left me.

"My goddess calls me to make this sacrifice, and I do so gladly. I've lived many lifetimes already. Citla Zaniyah proved that a queen can be born, even if you don't know how you came to be. Your goddess has other plans for your house, and I don't believe your sacrifice will be required, unless you will it so."

"But how can I have a child when I never breed?"

Ironically, Aima queens fed on blood, but over the millennia, we'd lost the ability to menstruate. We had so few queens left, which meant fewer strongholds where Aima could live under a queen's protection. Only a queen could breed another queen, but we couldn't have children at all. Let alone ensure the continuation of our long lineages with a daughter.

"Your mother accomplished much to have you, and she rejuvenated your family's bloodline in you, but my guess is you'll need a god's power to conceive."

A god…

"Who's my father?" I whispered. "A god?"

She sighed softly, swirling around me, her hair a black silken cloud. "I believe so. An ancient god of great power. But how or who she might have found, only you can discover."

Mama never had Blood of her own, protectors sworn to guard her as their queen. She'd never even formally been the Zaniyah queen. After a horrific attack when she was a young woman, Mama had barely spoken for days and weeks at a time. She'd only rarely gone anywhere outside our nest. She'd been too afraid.

Yet somehow, she'd not only managed to conceive, but to also deliver a healthy baby girl blessed with our goddess's power. While powerful queens like my friend had tried every spell known to Aima courts and still failed to conceive a daughter.

"Prepare your nest first." She wrapped her arms around me, flooding me with her sweet scent. I could feel her strength in her arms and the heat of her body. Yet I had no idea who she was. "Call as many Blood as you can. Make your nest as secure as possible."

I clutched her, blinking back tears. "It's too late. Keisha Skye has already cursed my nest. No queen will come to our aid. Do I dare have a child, when I can't ally myself with any queen other than her?"

She pulled back and looked into my eyes, her beautiful

face hardening. Her eyes glittered like shards of obsidian. "Whatever you do, do not allow your nest to fall to House Skye. Keisha is tampering with dark magic to gain an heir. She'll want to claim your house so she can study your blood-line and try to duplicate whatever your mother did to conceive you. You must stay free and out of Skye's control."

"I'm stronger, thanks to your teachings, but nowhere near strong enough to stand against the queen of New York City."

"You won't have to stand against her alone."

"But—"

She gave me another hug, her smile transforming from fierce to secretive. "You will have assistance when you need it."

"I will? But who? If you're gone…"

She kissed my cheek and backed away, fading like a ghost, or a figment of my imagination. "My daughter will come when you need her most. She will stand against even the Triune for those she loves."

I OPENED my eyes and touched my cheek. I could still feel the petal-soft touch of her lips on my skin and smell her scent of jasmine and vanilla. But her name…

Squeezing my eyes shut, I concentrated fiercely. *Who are you? What is your name? Who is your daughter? When will she come?*

Wind swirled through the open windows, carrying the tinkling of chimes. A nightingale sang from the avocado tree that grew by the kitchens. I thought I heard soft laughter mixed in with the chimes, but it might have only been my imagination.

"My queen?" My alpha, Eztli, whispered beside me. "Are you well?"

His big palm was warm and soothing on my shoulder. I rolled to him and he pulled me tightly against his chest, his heartbeat loud and steady beneath my cheek. "I'm fine. It was just a dream."

"The unknown queen again?"

I nodded, rubbing my mouth against his skin. "I wish I knew who she was."

He'd been the first Blood I'd called, and for many years, my only protector. Since Mama never had Blood, I'd never tried to call my own. I didn't think I was strong enough. But the woman in my dreams said he was out there, desperately waiting for me to call him.

She'd been right. As soon as I knew what to look for, I felt him miles to the south, prowling the jungle in his jaguar form. He was everything I'd ever wanted: strong, loyal, kind, steadfast, and a large part of my heart that I'd never known was missing. He easily stepped into the role of my alpha Blood, helping to protect the nest and my family, though I was always his primary concern.

I couldn't imagine life without him. Yet in over a hundred years of wonderful sex, he'd never been able to give me a child. I'd never even had my period, the first sign of a breeding queen. My alpha would give me the moon and stars if he could. To know that I wanted a daughter, and he couldn't provide one...

It broke my heart to feel his guilt. To know that he felt like such a failure, when I loved him so very much.

"What did she say this time?"

I didn't want to tell him. I didn't want to make him feel worse. "I need to find out who my father was."

"Surely Tocih knows."

I shook my head, turning it into a caress, my lips sliding over his skin. "I asked Grandmama many times as a child, and she said she never knew. I gave up asking, because in the end, it didn't matter to me."

His fingers combed through my hair, a slow stroke that didn't tangle or pull my hair once. Goddess, he was so tender. So gentle. Why couldn't he be the one to give me the heir we needed? "Yet it matters now, after the dream."

I curled tighter against him, trying to shield him from the truth. "She said I ought to know."

Silent a few minutes, he continued to stroke my hair. His chest rumbled beneath my face, a low purr rolling from his throat. His scent filled my nose, stirring my hunger. Sleek, powerful jaguar, the mighty jungle hunter, silently gliding through the deepest jungles in search of prey. I could smell his fur and the lush greenery of the jungle, as if he'd crept through ferns and branches to reach me.

My hunger was more than just a need for blood, though yes, as an Aima queen, I needed his blood to enhance my power. I yearned for the jungle. A thousand scents on the air, from rich loam to sweet fruits. The air heavy with dampness, heat, and the scent of frantic growth. Everything was either trying to grow taller to find the sun above the canopy—or adjusting to life below the trees in near darkness.

An apt metaphor for my life. I wanted more power, yes. I *needed* more power, or I wouldn't be able to hold my nest against the Keisha Skyes of the world. I wouldn't be able to keep my Blood. Yet if I blindly rushed to the top of the canopy in search of the sun…

I would miss this. The quiet comfort of my alpha's arms around me.

"Why is your father important?" Eztli whispered.

I closed my eyes, even though he couldn't see my face. I wouldn't lie to him. Ever. And not telling him…

It was the same as a lie. Even if the truth would hurt him.

"She thinks my father was a god."

My alpha was many things, including extremely clever, for a man, at least.

He huffed out a breath of amusement, picking up my thought in our bond. "That's how your mother was able to conceive you."

I remained silent, letting him put the pieces together in his own time. I felt the exact moment he realized why it was important to me. A heavy weight sagged in our bond, as if all of Tenochtitlan had been built on top of his heart. Tears pooled in my eyes, but I didn't cry. I wouldn't hurt him even more by crying. He hated my tears.

His fingers never ceased stroking my hair. "Which god will you claim to sire your heir, my queen?"

2

MAYTE

The next morning, I started looking for my quarry. I needed answers, even if they weren't answers that I necessarily wanted to hear.

As the former Zaniyah queen, Grandmama still had enough power that she sensed my intention to seek her out, and so she made herself scarce. I could have tapped my power and found her easily, but I didn't want to make her feel lesser than me in any way. I was queen of our Zaniyah nest now, but I existed purely because she'd taken care of me and had managed to keep us all alive until I grew strong enough to help.

Any time she thought of those early years, her eyes took on a haunted look, as if dark memories tumbled through her mind. Which told me that my mysterious friend was probably right. Grandmama had to suspect who my father was and had kept it secret all this time.

She wouldn't give up that information without a damned good reason.

When even my twin brothers had no idea where Grandmama was, I knew to look for her out back in what I fondly called her witch hut. Her last alpha, Hernando, had built a shed behind the kitchens for her many years ago. She called it her gardening shed, but my skin tingled and my scalp itched as I neared it. She was working her magic.

Grandmama had always told me that she wasn't like other queens, which was one reason she liked our seclusion and general anonymity among the Aima courts. She didn't like formality or politics, but preferred the simple, quiet country life. More, she liked to dabble in potions and spells that went beyond blood magic. I had no idea if the kind of magic she worked was typical of other queens or not.

Her potions worked extremely well, though the ones she'd given me for fertility over the years had done nothing to bring about my menses.

I tapped on the door and waited several moments before she finally said, "Come in, child."

I slipped inside and shut the door behind me. She liked her privacy, and though no one in the nest would ever dare step foot inside this hut without her permission, she'd hopefully talk more freely if we were alone and hidden from prying eyes.

It took a few moments for my eyes to adjust. The hut had no windows, and the only light in the room was an old-fashioned lantern. A high table stood in the center of the room, and the walls were lined with shelves filled with jars and boxes, all carefully labeled. Dried roots, feathers, and special animal bones hung from the rafters, low enough for her to reach them as she needed. I was several inches taller than her, so I paid careful attention to the hanging bundles to avoid hitting my head.

She had an assortment of jars open in front of her. A small pot bubbled away on a portable propane burner. I didn't need to look at the ingredients to know that she was working on a healing potion. I could feel it in the way my magic responded to hers.

Like her, I didn't have to bleed to work my healing or earth magic. We saved our blood magic for the truly desperate and powerful spells. When there was no other way to save a life or protect our nest, we bled, gladly. The Zaniyah queens were tightly bound to the land and plants. Our crops were always abundant and large. The rains came when they were needed. Our people stayed healthy.

Because we bled to make it so.

Well, I did, now. Grandmama only offered her blood once a year to make sure our blood circle remained solid, especially with Keisha Skye's geas laid on top of our nest.

Silently, I helped her with small tasks. Stirring the pot, putting the jars back in their correct locations, retrieving a sterile jar for her concoction. I'd helped her countless times over the years, so we worked well together without instruction.

She turned the flame off to allow the potion to begin cooling and let out a sigh. "I don't know who your father is. Not for sure."

"But you suspect."

She gave me a single nod, though she avoided my gaze. "I'm sorry, child, but silence was the only way to protect you. If I'm right…"

Grandmama had always been a formidable woman, even with her elderly stature. Now, though, she looked fragile and small. Her shoulders were hunched against a chill I could not feel. Her face was lined from horrors I had never faced.

I went around the table and put my arms around her, both for comfort and protection. She trembled with strain against me, and worry squeezed my throat. We Aima were hardy and lived for hundreds of years without issue, but I suddenly felt every single one of her many centuries. "I'm sorry, I know this is troubling you. I'm not questioning your reasoning or blaming you for hiding anything, because I know you were protecting me. But if we want another Zaniyah heir, I need to know how Mama conceived me."

Grandmama exhaled, and the tension shimmering in her slight body relaxed. "I always told you that Citla passed away when you were born, which is true. But she didn't die in childbirth. I allowed you to believe that was the case, though that might have made you feel guilty as a child."

She turned in my arms and reached up to cup my face in both her hands. Gnarled with age and hard work, her hands squeezed me firmly, her gaze locked to mine. "Hernando and I found Citla in the cenote the morning after she delivered you. She'd drowned."

I blinked, my mind buzzing helplessly in random circles. Suicide. But why? The cenote was miles away, but she could have made it on foot in an hour or so. Why there? If she'd wanted to kill herself, she could have drowned in the grotto. Unless she'd needed the fall to make sure she was successful. The cliff walls of the cenote were at least thirty feet above the water, and no one knew how deep the water actually was.

In fact, some people believed the cenote was bottomless. They said...

My eyes flared wide and I clutched her hands to my face, searching her gaze.

"She believed that she could pass through," Grandmama whispered, her low voice intent. "She was trying to reach her lover."

Her lover.

My father.

Through a cenote.

My brain floundered a moment. "The stories..."

She nodded, still holding my gaze.

In the old days, humans had sometimes sacrificed things

—including people—to the gods by throwing them into the cenote, because they believed the water was a portal to the otherworld. A portal directly to the gods.

It made a dreadful kind of sense why Mama might have tried to reach her unnamed lover through the cenote. But if she'd drowned, she hadn't been successful. So how had he found her in the first place?

"About eight months before you were born, Citla disappeared for two days. It'd been a long, terrible winter, and she seemed to be withering. Pale and listless, she barely moved or ate unless I fed her every bite myself. When we finally had a beautiful sunny day that spring, Hernando helped me move her outside, and she beamed with joy at the sun. Every day that we made sure she went outside, she got better and seemed so much happier.

"One day in May, I was in the garden working, and she sat on a blanket beneath the avocado tree. I remember seeing a bird dancing around her, but I thought nothing of it. She had a special way with animals. Even as a child, she'd healed many a broken wing and rescued baby bunnies from the dogs. I carried a basket of vegetables into the kitchen, and when I came back, she was gone. I looked for her myself but couldn't find her anywhere in the nest. I called Hernando, and he shifted to his jaguar and followed her scent, but he lost it a few paces outside the nest."

"What kind of bird was it?" I asked hoarsely.

"A hummingbird."

I closed my eyes. Of course. No wonder she hadn't told me. "Hummingbird on the Left."

Even here in the darkness of her hut, I didn't trust saying the Aztec sun god's true name out loud. Huitzilopochtli was the patron god of Tenochtitlan, where my family had lived before the fall of the Aztec Empire in 1521. Mainly known as the god of war, he was also associated with sunlight. Once,

I'd even heard one of Grandmama's sibs humming an ancient hymn to him. *"See him glitter. See him shine."*

At the height of Tenochtitlan, it was nothing for hundreds of prisoners and captives to be sacrificed to him.

Hundreds.

The temple steps had run red with the blood of his sacrifices.

My father.

According to whispered rumors, at some point, he'd joined Ra, the Egyptian god of light, or perhaps been absorbed by him. None of us really knew for sure. But there was only one sun god now, and he was hellbent on destroying every single Aima queen. Our nests would be destroyed, our houses broken. Forever.

So why would the god of light father a child on an Aima queen?

"She couldn't, or wouldn't, tell me where she had been," Grandmama whispered. "But she was glowingly happy. She talked more. She went on walks, both inside and outside the nest. What could I do? She was an adult, and though she'd never been right after the nightmare at Tocatl's nest, I was relieved that she was coming out of her shell. I'd never seen her so active and present. She told me she was in love, and that he would be coming back for her soon.

"She often sat outside in the full noonday sun and talked to him. Whether he heard her or not, I don't know. She told him she was pregnant with his child. She told him she was ready to leave with him."

Grandmama's voice broke, and she wiped her eyes with her apron. "She swore he'd come for her at the summer solstice, but he didn't. Month after month passed, and she started to wither again. The weather matched her mood, and I thought she was manipulating the weather, though she'd never had that power before. We had hurricane after hurricane the rest of the summer, followed by weeks of blistering heat and no rain. The bugs were awful. Spiders as big as dinner plates crawled out of the jungle, pushing your dear mother over the edge. She couldn't bear the sight of spiders, not after surviving the horrors in the Great Goddess's domain.

"I feared daily that she would lose you. I could feel your magic already. I knew you were a queen, if only she could carry you long enough to let you survive. She delivered you four weeks early, and though you were small, you were healthy and strong enough to survive."

Tears trickled down my cheeks. My throat ached as if a giant had wrapped his fist around my neck and strangled me. "Did… she not want… me?"

"Oh, no, dearest child, she loved you. She asked me to take you outside and hold you up to the sun and declare you his. To proclaim you both his heir and ours. She swore he'd hear. You were born in the night, and by the time dawn came, she was gone. She left me a note, but all it said was 'I'm going to find him and bring him to see his daughter.'"

Only to die in the cenote.

"When we found her, I knew I could never announce you as his heir. Not like she'd intended. I couldn't risk you. As the years passed, I began to suspect so much. He never came to her call, and it definitely seemed like every force of nature was turned against our family that summer. Maybe those weather events weren't a new power she'd gained, but his attempt to wipe us out. The spiders especially tormented Citla. Only someone who knew her history would know what they'd do to her mental state. To this day, I believe the sun god was trying to kill her before she could have you. Or maybe he never knew about you in particular—but wanted Citla dead, for whatever reason. Because once she was gone, the strange attacks stopped."

My heart felt painful and swollen, as if my rib cage had tightened like a vise. I swallowed and took a deep breath. Then another. At least now I knew, though I had no idea what to do with such knowledge. What did it change?

In the end, it didn't matter who my father was. Only *what* he was.

A god.

As a child, I'd built incredible fantasies about my father. He'd come riding in on a snorting black stallion to carry me away. Or fly into the nest like a massive fire-breathing dragon. I yearned to know him and my mother. At least I had Grandmama's stories about Citla, but I'd never had a single story or clue about my father. Even a child's wildest imagination hadn't conjured the sun god as my true sire.

Fear curdled my stomach, my brain whirling frantically. What if I stepped outside and Huitzilopochtli struck me down? Or he sent a horde of spiders to torment me like my poor mother? I wasn't as deathly afraid of them as she was, but the last thing I'd want to fight off was a giant spider.

But so much still didn't make sense. I knew more now, definitely, but why would he want my mother dead? Why would he impregnate her in the first place, if he was going to try and kill her?

"What now?" I whispered.

"First, you're going to give this potion to Felipa to fix the black rot on her roses," Grandmama said tartly as she pushed the jar into my hand. "Then, you're going to call more Blood."

I took a deep breath and slowly let it out. Yes. I had the capacity to call more Blood to me. Eztli had been with me the longest, and I'd called Maxtla and Luis later as I continued to gain in power. Each of them fed me regularly and deeply, increasing my power.

The more power I had, the more Blood I could call. It was an important cycle for the ruling queen of the nest. Especially if I wanted to breed the next Zaniyah heir. "And then I need a god."

Grandmama snorted. "Not just any god will do for you, child."

A slow smile spread on my face, and I laughed softly. "You're right. I need a jaguar god, don't I? So how does one go about finding a long-dead jaguar god that no one even remembers anymore, let alone believes in?"

Grandmama patted my cheek. "You call him, of course. And then you take him."

3

MAYTE

Night enfolded me as I walked the Zaniyah lands beyond the nest's blood circle.

Trees grew thicker and taller, so old and majestic they might have sprouted before Grandmama was even born. The moon was just a silver slip in the sky, but millions of stars twinkled and blinked, a secret language that I couldn't quite understand. Staring up at the midnight sky, I felt the answer inside me, even though I didn't quite understand in words what the universe, or the goddesses, were trying to tell me. I felt it in my bones and in the pulse of magic in my blood.

Now.

It's time.

Three jaguars prowled through the underbrush, though the biggest stayed close enough to me that his tail touched my thighs. Eztli always remained close, even as his jaguar. My fangs descended, and he made a low, coughing grunt of hunger. I held my wrist out to him and let him tear open my skin.

Power rumbled to life inside me. I didn't shift to his form

—I couldn't. Shifting into a jaguar had never been my gift, only the ability to call them to my side. However, I did gain his enhanced senses. I could suddenly see perfectly in the dark shadows beneath the trees. I could tell the difference between the squeaks of bats feeding on the ripe fruit overhead and the tiny mice shuffling through the leaves on the ground. The slight rasp of a snake's coils as it hunted its prey rang in my head as clearly as a bell. Thousands of scents flooded me, carrying all the messages of the land and its inhabitants. The jungle filled me, each life a blip on an internal radar that spun out into the night.

Eztli cradled my wrist in his formidable jaws, letting my blood run down his throat. His tongue was like sandpaper, but it was a rasp that I enjoyed. The rough stroke of his tongue told my body he was feeding, and soon, he'd be feeding me.

:Enough,: I told him in our bond, and he immediately released me. I needed blood for the call, and I didn't want to bleed so much that he had to carry me home.

I held my wrist out so that my blood dripped onto a stele of crumbling stone that was almost hidden by thick ferns. So many lost cities lay buried in these jungles. Pyramids, temples, and ball courts from generations so long ago that even Grandmama didn't know the cities. I wasn't sure which goddess's image was carved into the worn rock, but it didn't matter. In my mind, it was Coatlicue, the Mother of the Gods, our Zaniyah patron.

She stirred in my mind. Approval flowed through me like a touch of coolness in an otherwise warm pool of water. I had never seen Her directly, though I felt Her touch and influence in my life often. Grandmama said I didn't want to meet Her, because She only called us to Her pyramid home, Coatepec or "Snake Mountain", when She had a dire purpose.

When someone needed to die.

I didn't have death on my mind tonight. Only life and power. Blood and sex.

My usual thoughts, to be honest. The stronger I was, the better protected House Zaniyah would be, and blood was the path to greater strength. Inevitably, sharing blood led to sharing bodies too, and the more I shared with my Blood, the deeper and richer our bonds became.

My sacrifice sent a ripple of power through the old ruin. Letting my blood fall as it may, I walked up a fern covered hill, that was actually a small, overgrown temple. The jungle had swallowed it up, but the stones were still there, as well as the ancient power.

Sacrifice had been offered here many times before. Whether or not humans had lost their lives, priests always sacrificed their blood to the gods. Blood opened the portal to the otherworld. Absently, I wondered if Mama had known she needed to bleed in order to try and open the cenote portal, or if she'd just jumped in. I'd have to ask Grandmama if she knew.

On the flattened peak of the pyramid, I spread my arms, tipped my head back, and just breathed. I soaked in the jungle and let my mind roam the night. I touched each of my jaguar Blood briefly, their purrs and low roars familiar and dear to me. Not even thirty paces away, I felt a wild jaguar, wholly animal with no Aima blood. She crouched high above a game trail on a heavy limb, the glow of her eyes the only hint of her presence. Her coat blended in perfectly with the dark shadows and moonlight dappling through the canopy.

She inclined her head to me, and I knew she would do my bidding if I asked. But she was not Blood to be called.

I let my awareness spread further, lightly touching the other nocturnal beasts in the trees. Focusing on my need, I whispered aloud, "Come to me, my jaguar Blood, wherever you may be. Your queen has need of you."

The night breeze carried my intent out into the world like a tumbling leaf. Powered by my blood, my call rose in strength. With my three jaguars pressing against me, I drew on their strength as well. Eztli's unswerving loyalty. Maxtla's fatalistic warrior attitude. He'd fought the tide of Spaniards and lost our greatest city, yet he lived to fight another day. Luis burned with the need for retribution. His brother had died decades ago, before he'd come to me, but Luis still hunted the beast who'd managed to kill a young but powerful jaguar shifter.

If we were going to leave the nest in search of my jaguar god, I needed as many Blood as possible. The god I sought was Tezcatlipoca, or Smoking Mirror. The god of darkness, divination, and earthquakes. But I had chosen him because of the other form he took in our religion, his jaguar aspect, Tepeyollotl, or Mountain Heart. Even his name sent a thrill through my power, a zing of confirmation that yes, he was the one.

He was the god for me.

Far to the south, I felt a slight tug, as if a fly had brushed the furthest edge of a massive web. My heart leaped with excitement. Could a long-lost god truly be found so easily?

I reached toward that distant sense of something… important. He was miles and miles away. Not the god, sadly, but a jaguar Blood. I felt him running through the dense jungle, his sleek body stretched out in flying leaps to reach me as soon as possible.

Good. Hopefully four Blood would be enough protection to risk leaving the nest in search of Tepeyollotl.

I turned in a slow circle, fingers spread wide to pick up the slightest sense of anything else responding to my call. Blood trickled down to my elbow, but I sensed nothing else. Not even a glimmer of Tepeyollotl, though I wasn't sure what a jaguar god would even feel like. Pausing, I offered my other wrist to Maxtla and allowed him to feed for a few moments before allowing my blood to drip onto the ancient stone.

"Coatlicue, Great Mother, Skirt of Snakes, please hear Your child's plea. Show me where Tepeyollotl rests. Help me find my future daughter's father. Help us continue Your line in House Zaniyah."

My instincts were to strain and push for any clue, but generally, that wasn't the way my goddess worked. She much preferred a quiet, peaceful submission to Her will. I needed to surrender, so She could work *through* me, not *for* me.

It wasn't in my nature to wait quietly. I wanted to be busy. I wanted to make lists and plot maps and call every Aztec and Mayan expert to ask them where they thought a long-lost god's final resting place might be. I was a doer. A fixer. A planner.

But none of those things would help me find Tepeyollotl.

I bled until my knees trembled and my head buzzed, but I felt nothing other than the new Blood far to the south.

Sighing, I drooped against Eztli's side, and he bumped his giant head against my stomach. *:You must have patience, my queen. Tenochtitlan wasn't built in a single day.:*

I wrapped my arm over his shoulder to steady myself as I carefully climbed down from the pyramid. Offering blood had never failed me before. I wasn't sure what else to try. Maybe one of Grandmama's potions?

Luis bounded ahead of us, scouting the path for anything or anyone who might threaten me. *:The god you seek is called Smoking Mirror for a reason.:*

"I know," I replied slowly. "What does that mean?"

:You're too young to remember the old ways,: Maxtla replied. *:In Tenochtitlan, his priests used polished obsidian mirrors to speak to him.:*

Hope quickened my pace back to the nest. "I'll see if

Grandmama has one. She has everything else hoarded away somewhere."

:Tomorrow,: Eztli growled, his bond firming in my mind.

I knew he was only trying to take care of me, but I didn't want to seem weak. A queen should probably toss her head with a haughty laugh and make a defiant statement, but he was right. I was exhausted, and I had to be smart and stay within my limits.

I needed to feed. I needed to rest.

And then I would search the nest top to bottom for an obsidian mirror.

Whatever that was.

4

EZTLI

I held my queen as she slept, fighting to loosen my grip on her so she could gain the rest she needed.

My jaguar paced back and forth inside me, snarling and lashing his tail. *She's my queen. I will fight for her. I will die for her.*

Closing my eyes, I pressed my face into the curve of her neck so I could breathe her scent of dragon fruit and honeysuckle. Her sweet, flowery scent usually calmed me, but tonight, it threatened to push me over the edge.

Alphas were always in control, not just of the other Blood, but of ourselves. I'd never had difficulty reining in my predatory instincts before, but tonight, all I wanted to do was tear my competition apart.

Even Maxtla's soft panting was like an annoying pest buzzing in my ears. He'd stretched out on the balcony railing, surveying our queen's territory and ready to pounce at the first sign of trouble. I still remembered the day he'd answered her call. He'd sat outside the blood circle, waiting for an invitation to approach. There hadn't been a moment's doubt in me as I stared back at him. I didn't shift to my jaguar to challenge him.

I knew. He knew.

I was Mayte Zaniyah's alpha. Without question.

Now a single question plagued me, driving me towards insanity.

Would I still be alpha if she claimed a god so she could sire her heir?

A fucking god.

How was an alpha Blood supposed to deal with not only another man in his queen's bed, but a supremely powerful immortal being as old as time itself?

I'd never felt a moment's jealousy when she asked other Blood to her bed. She allowed me to remain near in case she needed me, but she generally preferred to take us one at a time. I didn't mind. I was alpha. I knew I could send any of the others away with a push of my beast's formidable will.

I could not send a god away from her. Even as queen, *she* might not have the power to do so. I loved her dearly, and I would die before I allowed anyone to harm one hair on her head, but she wasn't a kick-ass fighter. She didn't care to play politics or seek more power for her court. All she wanted was for her nest to be safe and for her people to live happily, as we had been for centuries.

And a daughter. Her greatest and most desperate want. The only thing I could not provide to her.

If a blight attacked the crops or illness struck your family, she was the queen to call. She could heal almost anything. But I had no idea how she'd be able to bend a god to her will. She simply wasn't powerful enough.

If he hurt her…

What could I do, but sacrifice myself trying to protect her? What could any of us do?

Luis touched my mind. *:The new Blood has arrived.:*

:Bring him through the circle and let him come to her.:

I carefully began untangling myself from her limbs. As I slid to the edge of her bed, she sleepily raised her head.

"Eztli?"

"Your newest Blood is here, my queen."

Her eyes widened, and she sat up. "So quickly? I swear he felt like he was in Guatemala, or perhaps even further south."

The new man paused in the doorway, waiting to be acknowledged. At least he seemed to have manners and sense, though his chest heaved with exertion. He smelled like a rank male in rut, and a raw, desperate light burned in his gaze, though he didn't challenge me. He was quick to salute with a fist to his heart and even inclined his head. "Alpha."

"Welcome to House Zaniyah." My voice was rougher than I intended. I couldn't seem to get my jaguar fully under control. "What's your name?"

"Diego Chak."

I gestured toward Mayte's bed, but I didn't look at her. I didn't want her to see that same rawness reflected in my own eyes, though it was for an entirely different reason. "Our queen, Mayte Zaniyah, daughter of Coatlicue."

Diego moved closer to her bed. "My queen. I'm yours. Use me as you see fit."

Her hunger tugged on me like an incessant tide. I waited at the door, hoping she might call me back to bed. She did sometimes, though she usually preferred to have only one man's full attention. I hated this desperation and helpless rage. It wasn't her fault. She must have an heir. I understood her desire to have a daughter, and supported her wish with all of my heart and soul.

But why couldn't *I* be the one to fulfill her heart's desire?

The new man let out a rumbling roar, and I knew she'd sank fangs into him. Without calling me back to her side.

Quietly, I stepped outside and shut the door behind me.

My jaguar roared and thrashed inside me with the force of his fury. He wanted to race like a killing wind through the night and release this anger on any hapless thrall or demon that might have stumbled near Zaniyah lands.

But with a queen so tightly bound to her land, few monsters dared come too close. It was impossible to hide from her, and so it was impossible to hide from me. If I hunted with this anger burning in me, I'd kill an innocent creature out roaming the night, and it would be a waste. I didn't need meat.

I needed my queen.

A soft groan escaped me, and I tipped my head back against the door. Maybe the jaguar god would kill me. Then I wouldn't have to live without ever touching my beloved queen again.

5

MAYTE

Since my alpha had come to me, I could count on one hand the number of mornings I woke without Eztli beside me. Today was one of them. I touched his bond and felt him in the hallway, dressed and ready for my call.

But he didn't feel... right. Only a few feet paces separated us physically, but his bond felt as distant as the stars.

I didn't prod and invade his privacy. That wasn't my way, though I certainly could have cracked his stoic silence open like a walnut. I was his queen, the air he breathed and the source of his power. If I gave him an order, he'd do it, compelled by my blood and magic flowing through his veins.

As a young woman, I'd realized that becoming the Zaniyah queen would carry so many heavy responsibilities. I'd expected to take care of our family, but I had no idea that I would have such impressive and powerful men at my beck and call—men whom I could crush with an impetuous thought. I knew that it would wound his pride and destroy our relationship if I forced the issue. He had to come to me willingly.

When he wanted to discuss this problem with me, he would. Besides, it was easy enough to guess what was bothering him so much that he'd walled himself off from me.

One new Blood had already arrived, and the jaguar god I needed to find loomed on the horizon like a dark, unknown storm that could devastate everything we'd built together. I didn't know what would happen when I found Tepeyollotl. I simply had no idea. Would he be glad to be discovered? Or furious? Would he sire my daughter and then be done with me? Would he try to kill my Blood?

I closed my eyes for a moment, inwardly shuddering with horror. It could happen. I had to acknowledge and face that fear. It would devastate me if anything happened to my Blood because of the steps I took to have the child I so desperately wanted.

Yet what choice did I have?

I turned and looked at the man I'd taken last night. His hunger had been great, in more ways than one. I'd loved his wildness, his desire raging out of control toward violence. There wasn't anything quite as exciting as taking a new Blood that very first time after he'd wandered aimlessly for so long in search of a queen. It was the only time any of my Blood had ever even come close to hurting me.

His eyes still burned with need, as if he wanted nothing more than to fuck me again. His hair was as rumpled as my bed and sexy as hell. I wanted to comb my fingers through the long strands that hung down into his eyes. Maybe to tidy him up, or better yet, to muss him up even more.

But I had too much to do to lie in bed making love all day. It definitely wouldn't feel right to make Eztli wait outside and listen, either. Especially not with this tension shimmering between us.

I did lean down and brush a kiss against my new Blood's lips, but I kept it light and withdrew before he could wrap his arms around me. "Thank you for coming to my call. What's your name?"

"Diego, my queen, formerly of House Chak."

My eyes widened. Chelle Chak was a queen of the old guard, one of Grandmama's friends when she'd been queen. Grandmama and Chelle were sibs, but I had never formalized such a relationship with her. "Her nest is in Antigua. How did you get here so quickly?"

He slipped from my bed and padded around the room as quietly as his jaguar. One moment he was at the balcony, and the next, he was coming back in through the door to the hallway. My balcony was on the second floor of the house. In the back of the house. He would have had to race around to the front of the house and back up the stairs. In the blink of an eye.

"I can move great distances in a single step. It's as though space has no hold on me."

Awed, I tried to estimate the miles between us when I'd first made the call last night. He'd crossed the jungles and mountains from Guatemala to Zaniyah lands in Mexico in a matter of hours. By foot. Or paw, rather. It was astounding.

"My apologies, my queen. That's why I was so ravenous last night."

"No wonder. That's quite a miraculous gift. Please let me know when your reserves are running low."

He inclined his head. "Normal food also helps restore my body's energy. By your leave, I'll sniff out the kitchen and grab some food."

"Of course. Sarah's an excellent cook. I'll be along shortly."

I'd nearly finished dressing when Grandmama suddenly spoke in my head. *:I have something to show you in the attic.:*

She only rarely used our blood bond to communicate,

even though she'd fed me often enough as a child. *:I'll be right there.:*

I stepped outside, and Eztli nodded. "I heard."

Even his voice was tight, simmering with so much left unsaid. We walked upstairs in silence, my heart aching with every step. I hated this. I didn't want to hurt him, or, goddess forbid, lose him entirely. I didn't want our lives or relationship to change.

I sighed softly, shaking my head. Everything would change. A child would complicate even a regular human marriage. For a queen to sire an heir was even more important and exponentially more difficult. Even if everything went perfectly, our lives would still be in turmoil. The danger would be greater. Always.

That was why I needed to call Diego last night. That was why I needed to find the god. Even if he killed us all.

I laid my hand on the door knob to the small storage room tucked beneath the roof, but I hesitated. Looking at him, I let sincerity shine in my eyes. "I love you, Eztli."

His grim edge softened slightly, but he didn't smile. "And I love you, my queen."

I wanted him to say that all would be well. He would make it so. But he couldn't. He wouldn't lie to me, not even to make me feel better.

I pushed the door open and stepped into the attic. Dust motes danced in the air. Boxes were stacked here and there, mixed in with old furniture, picture frames, and other treasures from the past that Grandmama couldn't bear to part with. Thick dust covered most everything, making it easy for me to follow her tracks around a stack of old trunks.

She sat on a sheet-draped chaise lounge that had once been in Mama's room. On her lap, she held a rounded wooden case. It almost looked like a guitar case, though it was missing the long neck. As I neared, I could make out a calendar wheel as part of the design on the case, but I didn't recognize the other glyphs.

Patting the seat beside her, Grandmama silently invited me to sit. I did so, but she still didn't speak. She only stared at the case in her lap, her gnarled fingers tracing round and round the wheel.

I reached over and laid my hand on top of hers, stilling her aimless drawing. "What is it, Grandmama? What's wrong?"

"Nothing." She grimaced, shaking her head. "At least, not yet. I don't know if this is the right thing to do or not."

I had no idea what she might need to tell me. Why had she asked me to come to her, if she was afraid to give me whatever she'd found? I decided to talk about something else entirely until she was ready. "I called a new Blood last night."

She nodded but didn't reply.

"I went to the old ruin like last time. I bled so much that I could barely walk home, but I still couldn't find Tepeyollotl. I even asked for Coatlicue's help. I felt Her presence, but I have no idea where the god may be."

Grandmama blew out a sigh as she transferred the wooden case onto my lap. "That's what I was afraid of. I think this may help, but it's extremely dangerous."

Nothing fazed Grandmama, not even the giant spiders that were likely sent by the sun god to kill Citla before she could have me. So it must be especially dire. My fingers quivered as I flipped the latch and gingerly opened the case.

Inside, a white cloth lay on top of the item protected inside the case. Someone, likely Grandmama, had embroidered a dancing Aztec god in bold primary colors. Black and gold stripes crossed his face, and his right foot was replaced with a black circular disk. Something wiggled out from the circle, almost like snakes.

"I hoped you could call the jaguar aspect and not deal

with Tezcatlipoca directly, but I suppose you can't find one without the other." She touched the circular disk where his foot should be. "Smoking Mirror. He's the god of darkness, divination, and sorcery. He gave his priests obsidian mirrors, so they could view the supernatural and discover truths that would be impossible for mortals to learn on their own. They used the mirrors to not only talk to dead ancestors, but also to the god himself. If you're not careful, you can be sucked into the smoky world on the other side and lost forever, so you must respect it, every single time, and hold on firmly to what you love."

She pulled the cloth aside, and I saw myself looking back in the shiny black surface. Volcanic rock had been polished to a fine sheen.

"It's a mirror, so you see yourself first. You have to see and know yourself before the god will speak. You will see truths about yourself that may be difficult to face. Some people would rather not look, for fear of what they'll learn, and others have been driven mad, tormented by the truths they can't accept. It's impossible to lie to yourself in the obsidian mirror."

My fingertips were icy cold, and I gripped the outer case so tightly that my hands ached. I averted my gaze from the mirrored surface, my heart pounding. "How long do I have to look? How long is too long before it's dangerous?"

"Until you activate it with your blood, it's only a mirror. Other than that, I don't know. I've never used it myself." She lifted the mirror out of the case and lovingly ran her fingers around the unpolished rim. "It was my brother's."

She set it back in the case and dropped her hand over mine. I released my death grip on the case and entwined my fingers with hers. "Tupoc was one of Tezcatlipoca's teopixqui before the fall of the city. He smuggled as many holy items out of the temple as possible, including his obsidian mirror. I begged him to stay in the nest where we were safe, but he insisted on going back to Tenochtitlan. He said it wasn't over. The Spaniards would return despite their initial defeat, and he would die with his city. He told me to take everyone as far away from Tenochtitlan as possible, and that's how we came to our new lands here."

I squeezed her hand gently. "Did you ever see him use the mirror? Or did he tell you how to work it?"

She shook her head. "I don't know much more than I've already told you. I was called to the Templo Mayor once, when Mama was still alive, to help care for a young priest who'd been lost while using his mirror. Mama was the best healer I've ever seen, and even she said there was nothing anyone could do for him. His soul was already gone and his body died the next day."

"So, I might find the god I seek… and lose my soul at the same time. Great."

Grandmama snorted and released my hand to pat my cheek. "You're the queen of House Zaniyah and daughter of Coatlicue, Mother of the Gods. I think you'll do just fine. But I recommend extreme caution. Do all you can to locate his resting place before using the mirror, and if you must, use it rarely. Some people become so obsessed with the mirror that they can do nothing else but stare into it, lost in visions of the otherworld. Make sure your Blood are close by and able to pull you back if anything seems amiss. Use your intention, as you do when you work any magic. If our goddess wants another daughter, She'll help keep you safe."

My mind raced. If the mirror could help me find the god, then the risk would be worth it. I'd do anything to have a daughter, even risking my soul in the murky otherworld only priests had ever visited. "Where do you think he rests?"

"Aztlán, where the Mexica originated."

That wasn't much help, because no one knew where

Aztlán was located. Human researchers had been seeking the mythological city for as long as they'd been looking for Atlantis.

I carefully rewrapped the mirror and secured the case. "Is there a certain time of day I should try to reach him?"

"Never during the day. The night is Tezcatlipoca's domain."

Darkness. If I was truly Huitzilopochtli's child, then the last thing I wanted to do was work any magic in the light of day. I didn't want to draw his attention to me or the nest.

Let alone to my future child.

6

MAYTE

Twenty Years Later

I COULDN'T SEEM to stay warm outside of the nest. Even in December, the temperatures in Texas weren't that different from what we saw at home. It was the lack of safety and security that made me hunch my shoulders and hug myself. I wasn't actually cold, though my teeth did occasionally chatter. My nerves were getting the best of me. Though we went home periodically, these trips were taking a toll on me.

I'd been as meticulous in my research as any Mesoamerican expert hoping to make the discovery of the century. Over the years, I'd talked to anyone who'd ever written a paper or made a knowledgeable comment about Aztlán, the legendary origin of seven tribes, one of which migrated to Lake Texcoco and founded Tenochtitlan.

We'd made excursions to at least fifty different lakes, from western Mexico to New Mexico and now, to Texas. I needed a lake with an island. How hard could that be to find?

Evidently, it was impossible to find the *right* one. To be honest, I couldn't imagine that any of these highly commercialized fishing and boating attractions would ever host the lost city. There were very few "wild" places left in the southern United States. Surely if Aztlán were anywhere north of the border, someone would have found it already.

That was what I'd told myself thousands of times as I stared at the obsidian mirror's case, my stomach clenched with dread. I had promised Grandmama I'd explore every reasonable location first before attempting to use the mirror as a last resort.

The last resort was upon me. All I had to show after all these years was a laptop full of notes and a stack of maps with big red Xs, only this time, X did not mark the spot where Tezcatlipoca lay in eternal sleep, but the sites I'd visited, and ultimately eliminated, as possibilities.

After examining yet another tourist-trap island resort near Austin, I'd despaired of ever finding a solid clue to Aztlán's location. Rather than driving all night, I asked Eztli to pull off the road so we could relax and sleep. We stopped at the first highway motel for a cheap room and ordered a stack of delivery pizzas. Half dozing, half watching the news, I almost missed it.

I shot out of bed so quickly that Maxtla and Luis both shifted to jaguar, while Eztli scooped me up in his arms, braced and ready to carry me to safety.

"No," I gasped, twisting back around to see the television. "Turn it up!"

Diego grabbed the remote control that had been knocked under the bed in our mad scramble, and rewound a few minutes so that I could hear the whole thing.

The male reporter was interviewing a very excited woman, Dr. Ramona Torres, who held two pieces of chipped, broken obsidian.

"Pause it," I told Diego and he hit the button, so I could see the chunk of rock better. "Doesn't that look like it's carved?"

The television screen was too small to be certain, but I could barely make out weathered lines of a glyph. I didn't know many of the ancient symbols, but I did know that one, because it was my brother's name. Itztli. Obsidian.

"Go ahead and let it play."

"As reported earlier this summer, Lake Tawakoni has receded significantly over the past few years thanks to drought conditions across the state. But this time, the low waters were a good thing, right, Ms. Torres?"

"It's Dr. Torres, and yes, we never would have found these artifacts under normal lake conditions."

"Right, sorry, so what's so significant about these pieces that have been found?"

"This is obsidian. There are no volcanoes in Texas," she replied dryly. "These are also fairly large chunks that also show evidence of carving and craftsmanship."

"What do you think they were used for?"

She adjusted the two pieces in her hands so they fit together, forming about one third of a dinner platter.

Or an obsidian mirror like the one Grandmama had given me.

"I believe this was a piece of polished obsidian that priests used in rituals to communicate with the otherworld."

"Not Catholic priests." The man laughed, as if he'd made a joke.

Dr. Torres was not amused. I made a mental note to find wherever she taught and make a donation to her university's department.

"*Mexica* priests, possibly dated prior to Tenochtitlan's existence. I won't know for sure until I have it tested."

"Do you mean Aztecs?"

"No. They never called themselves Aztecs."

The reporter blinked several times, as if trying to come up with something clever to say. Rather than risking sounding like an idiot, he changed the subject. "Why would a priest carry this all the way from Mexico, so it could be discovered in a Texan lake, Ms. Torres?"

"Doctor," she corrected him again, firmly. Then she turned to the camera, and it was like she was looking straight into my eyes and speaking directly to me. "What if they started *here* and meant to carry it south?"

I opened my mouth to ask for my laptop, but Eztli placed it on my lap, open and ready for me. I Googled Lake Tawakoni and found it about an hour east of Dallas. "That's where we need to head in the morning, though it doesn't look like it has an island. I never would have thought to check this lake as a possibility."

"It's big," he said over my shoulder. "Do you want us to try and locate Dr. Torres so you can speak to her?"

Already searching her name, I shook my head. "I found a transcript of the article. It says they found several items on the shoreline in the state park."

"That's still a lot of area to search, and this time of year, the park will likely be closed. At least we ought to be able to investigate as jaguars without worrying about being sighted by tourists."

A pulse of magic made my eyes flutter shut. I breathed deeply, letting my mind relax and open to the message from my goddess. She didn't speak words, but I felt Coatlicue's intent. Shivering, all I wanted to do was crawl under the cheap comforter and hide.

Eztli sat closely beside me and wrapped his arms around me. "What is it, my queen?"

I swallowed hard and cleared my throat. "I need to use the mirror."

"Now?" He asked softly, rubbing my back in soothing circles. "Or when we get closer?"

I leaned into him and buried my face against his throat. He held me, letting me soak in his heat and strength. My alpha had never failed me. *Goddess, please don't let me fail him. Especially now that I'm so close to finding the jaguar god.*

"When we're closer, I think. I'm hoping it will guide me to the exact location."

He pressed a kiss to the top of my head and tightened his arms around me. "At the first hint of trouble, I'll pull you back. I won't allow anything to harm you, not even Tezcatlipoca."

That was what I was afraid of.

Because if my Blood felt I was in danger, they'd die to protect me. Was I strong enough to protect them from a god?

7

EZTLI

My queen finally had a promising clue to the location of Aztlán after decades of fruitless searches. She could have her jaguar god in days, or even hours, if all went well.

I felt like utter garbage for wishing that all would *not* go well. It was a futile wish, and completely, despicably selfish. I was lucky to have found a queen at all, let alone one who'd loved me for so long.

But if this might be my last night with her as alpha, I would do everything in my power to ensure she would remember it always.

I didn't say anything, but I watched her with heavy-lidded eyes. Missing nothing. Holding back nothing in our bond. I studied her like a man who knew he'd soon lose his sight and needed to etch every facet of Mayte Zaniyah into my memory.

The exact dusky brown of her skin. The silky pink of her lips. The delicate curve of her ear as she tucked a wayward strand of hair back. When I'd first come to her call, she'd worn her mahogany hair bound in a braid and coiled at the base of her neck. I'd spent hours at a time simply brushing her hair and admiring the weight of it on my fingers. Every morning, I'd brushed and braided her hair, and every night when she took me to her bed, I'd unbraided and brushed it for her again.

Why did we stop that comforting ritual? I couldn't remember why she'd decided to cut her hair back to shoulder length years ago. But I missed it. I missed that small thing I could do to show her how much I loved her.

I still could have braided it for her, even though it was shorter. One day, she must have sent me to some small task and skipped our ritual. Which made it easy to skip again over the years.

I'd forgotten that simple pleasure.

Quietly, I rose and went to the small travel bag we'd placed in the bathroom for her. Aima didn't need shampoo or soap or even a toothbrush, but sometimes it was nice to have a small bag of toiletries available, especially around humans who wouldn't know what we were. Her wooden-handled brush was on top of a stack of rolled bandages and the small herbal first-aid kit that she liked to carry.

I undressed and left my clothes in the bathroom. She didn't notice as I came back into the room, too absorbed in studying the map of Lake Tawakoni in hopes of discovering another clue to the god's location. Her other three Blood had quietly withdrawn to the furthest edges of the small hotel room. Maxtla even had his hand on the doorknob, ready to step outside.

:*Stay*,: I told them all. :*Prepare yourselves.*:

Maxtla arched a brow at me in surprise but he didn't object, allowing his hand to fall away from the door.

I settled on the bed behind her, close enough to touch her,

though I didn't press my body against her. I carefully ran my fingers along her scalp, searching out the pins she'd used to hold her hair up off her neck. She hummed out a pleased little sigh, so I rubbed my fingertips more firmly, massaging her scalp and down the back of her neck.

Pin by pin, I released her hair and began to brush it. I started at the ends, holding them carefully in my left hand so I didn't pull a single strand. I took my time, slowly working the brush higher. Sometimes I gathered the heavy fall and brushed underneath, too, making sure to stimulate her scalp.

Over and over and over.

Her breathing slowed, her shoulders melting back against me. "That feels wonderful."

I set the brush aside and pushed my fingers up along the back of her head in long, firm strokes that loosened her muscles. "I'll braid it for you in the morning, if you'd like."

"Yes, I'd like that very much."

I continued the massage, turning my attention to her shoulders. Through our bond, I could feel the knot of tension over her right shoulder blade. She wasn't aware of the ache, not until I pressed my palm against the tenderness and carefully rubbed it away.

Muscle by muscle, she sagged against me, relaxed and completely at peace.

I raised my gaze to Maxtla and nodded.

He eased onto the bed and slipped her shoes off. Cradling her foot in his hands, he rubbed small circles along her sole. She groaned deep in her throat. "Goddess, that feels amazing."

"Let us take care of you, my queen," I whispered against her ear. "Let us love you. Please."

She reached up behind her and stroked her fingers over my jaw. "Yes."

I kissed her shoulder and slowly worked my mouth up the column of her throat. Her breath caught, and I felt her heartbeat quicken in our bond, waiting for me to kiss her in exactly the right place. After so many wonderful years together, I knew all the pleasure spots on her body, but I didn't rush. Maxtla matched my pace, gradually working his fingers up her calves, kneading his thumbs deeply into tense muscles while he kissed her ankles and rubbed his cheek against her knee.

I ran my tongue into the hollow behind her ear. Lightly nibbled her earlobe. Breathed into her ear as I whispered, "My queen. My one and only love."

She lifted her hips up off the bed, and Maxtla made short work of her jeans. She helped me pull the hoodie over her head. She hadn't worn a bra. I leaned back against the pillows, cradling her between my thighs, supporting her upper body as Maxtla made his way up to her pussy.

Even now, after making love countless times with each of us individually, a hint of pink darkened her cheeks as she looked up and saw Diego and Luis both watching us on the bed.

I kept my touch light as I massaged her shoulders, working away the sudden tenseness again. "They love you, too."

"I know. I just feel like I'm on display."

"Only for us. We only want to worship you."

I felt her hesitation tightening between us. She knew our hours could be numbered. She expected me to use that information to sway her will. She feared I would try to make her feel guilty for risking everything we had in order to find the jaguar god.

But I wouldn't ever hurt my queen. Even though it was true.

I might die tomorrow. We all might. Tezcatlipoca wasn't known for tenderness and compassion.

But I would willingly die this very moment if my queen asked it of me. I certainly wouldn't throw down accusations on her head.

Even if she ordered me to certain death.

Mayte

HE DESTROYED me with exquisite tenderness. How such a powerful man could be so gentle was a miracle to me. He had so many weapons at his disposal, but the most powerful one was the truth.

He could have told me the past twenty years had been a waste of time and effort. That I was obsessed with the impossible. I was determined to find something that no one in thousands of years had been able to locate. I had to be crazy to think that a minor, insignificant queen, unworthy of even the notice of the Triune, let alone a seat, would be able to find and subdue an ancient god of infinite power.

That I, Mayte Zaniyah, of no claim to fame or fortune, would be able to sire a child when nearly every queen for hundreds of years had failed.

My arrogance was likely to get us all killed, especially my Blood, who were sworn to protect me from all dangers. Even from an irate god that I dared poke and prod from his immortal sleep.

All true and valid accusations he could hurl at me.

Yet all he did was ask me to let him, and the rest of my Blood, make love to me. One last time.

My throat closed, thick with unshed tears. I didn't want

this to be our last time. I didn't want any of them in danger or hurt, let alone dead. Especially because of me.

"It's a risk we willingly accepted when we swore our blood to you," he whispered in my ear. His hands stroked my arms soothingly, drawing away my fear and guilt with a single touch. "We love you. That we had any time with you at all is a blessing from your goddess, and we thank you."

Maxtla was a big, burly warrior. I'd seen him rip a thrall apart with his bare hands down on the border. I'd never seen so many thralls as we did here in America. It was like they were insane with hunger, following our every step, even though they knew it would mean certain death. He could have gripped my thighs with those big, rough hands and forced his way into my body.

Buried deep inside me, a secret part of myself almost wished he would.

Yet he only stroked my skin like he'd never felt anything so fine and soft, waiting for me to decide. Would I let him in? Would I send him away? Would I send them all away and only take one, as I usually did?

I didn't know why it embarrassed me so much. Having multiple Blood at my side was a feat that queens in my family hadn't accomplished in generations. It was something to be extremely proud of, that I'd finally managed to call several Blood to my side, and I was strong enough to keep them all fed with my blood.

With my power.

And with my body.

Just knowing that they were all looking at me made my insides squirmy. It wasn't exactly unpleasant, just uncomfortable. I didn't like feeling so exposed and vulnerable. Like if they looked too deeply…

They might see something that would change their dedication to me. That I wouldn't be able to be their queen.

They didn't try to persuade or coerce me in any way. In fact, Maxtla started to pull away, sensing my unease.

I reached out and threaded my fingers into the thick curly fall of his hair, now streaked with silver. His face was worn and lined. He had never told me exactly how old he was, but I knew he'd been a warrior when Tenochtitlan fell. He'd been left for dead on the steps of Templo Mayor, with most of his right arm hacked off, and a gaping wound in his side.

Yet he'd lived. So he could find his way to me.

How could I send him away now, when he might die tomorrow to give me my heart's desire?

I opened my thighs, gently drawing him back to me. He wrapped his hands around my waist, bracing his forearms on my thighs, so he could bury his face against my stomach. He inhaled deeply, just holding me, as I held him.

Connection. Touch. Acceptance. All each of them had ever asked from me.

I combed my fingers through his hair and gently rubbed my fingers over his scalp, neck, and shoulders, massaging him as Eztli had done for me. Maxtla rolled his head back and looked up at me, his eyes dark with hunger. "May I feed from between your thighs, my queen?"

The taste of a queen's desire could have a powerful effect on her lover. Eztli had often made love to me with his mouth, using the aphrodisiac power to empty every drop of sperm in his body into me in the hopes that he could sire my daughter. We'd enjoyed it thoroughly, even though I never started breeding. But I'd never allowed any of my other Blood to do so.

:Do you mind?: I asked Eztli. On this, possibly our last night together before I found Tezcatlipoca, I didn't want to do anything to offend him.

:Of course not. I want all of your pleasure, my queen. Even if it's another giving that pleasure to you.:

I nodded to Maxtla, and he dipped his head to lightly trace his tongue between my thighs. He took his time, stroking every inch of me before settling in to suck and lick my clit. Eztli cupped my breasts, rolling my nipples between his fingers. I tried to be quiet, but the sensation of his fingers tugging and squeezing made me moan, which spurred Maxtla to stroke me more firmly with his tongue.

I forced my eyes open, and looked directly into Luis's smoldering gaze.

Heat flooded my face. He had crawled onto the bed with us. Closer, he prowled like a jaguar on the hunt. Holding my gaze as long as possible, he leisurely lowered his head to my nipple. Eztli even helped, lifting my breast up, offering it to him like a treat.

Luis's lips closed over my breast and Eztli's fingers, which were still rolling back and forth on my hardened flesh. I shattered and bucked against Maxtla's mouth, climaxing so hard that Eztli had to catch me, or I would have rolled off him to thrash on the mattress.

Another mouth closed over my other nipple, and I knew it was Diego. All four of my Blood. Touching me. Loving me. I couldn't hold back another hoarse cry.

Maxtla sank his fangs into my inner thigh, sending another wave of pleasure through me. My blood hummed in my veins, a crashing crescendo of need that thundered through my body. I felt like a tuning wand, vibrating from head to toe between them. Pleasure rippled through me, driving me higher, always higher.

I dragged Maxtla up into my arms and wrapped my thighs around him. Eztli held me, while my other Blood fucked me. They all held me, stroking me inside and out until the pleasure was a haze of color that filled my every sense. Maxtla roared with release, shuddering as he emptied hard into me.

Another took his place. Luis, or Diego, I couldn't tell with my eyes closed. I couldn't see or hear or think. But I focused on his scent and recognized Diego. His jaguar always smelled a bit wilder and rawer, as if no cage could ever contain him, not even my Blood's body.

Hunger surged in me, and I sank my fangs into his throat as he climaxed. I drank from him until Luis took his place and drove my pleasure higher.

Eztli. I needed my alpha. I wanted his blood. His pleasure.

I didn't need to ask him. He pulled me up and effortlessly turned me around to face him. He pushed up into me, holding me heart-to-heart. Tears dripped from my eyes, and I buried my face against his throat. I wanted to climb inside him and never leave. Let him hold me, like this, for all time.

He held me as long as possible without moving inside me, but I couldn't stop twitching and clenching around his cock. He filled me completely, a blissful fullness that made it impossible to simply lie connected and still. I didn't want to be still. I wanted him moving, driving me higher, pushing us both over the edge.

Deliberately, I tightened my muscles on him and sank my fangs into his throat. His back arched on a ragged groan. Instinct took over. His hips slammed up against me, lifting my knees up off the bed. I didn't care. I knew he wouldn't let me fall. His powerful arms locked around me, clutching me to him as we both climaxed.

One last time.

I refused to believe that. I refused to give him up. I refused to give up any of them.

I lifted my face, licking his blood from my lips. His eyes were dark with raw agony, moist with emotion. His bond raged like an angry volcano blasting its core thousands of feet into the air. "I'm not letting you go. Even to death and the otherworld."

He nodded, but the look in his eyes still cut me to the quick. "I will help you find your god. I will help you have your daughter. I swear it on your blood that burns inside me." He brushed his lips against me, so softly, despite his words. "Even if it kills me."

8

MAYTE

Eztli parked the Jeep in a deserted parking lot at the edge of Lake Tawakoni State Park, and Maxtla parked behind him. We could have all crowded into a single Jeep for this excursion, but if I was successful, we might have another person in the vehicle with us on the way back to the hotel. I had no idea what a god in the flesh would look like, but I guessed that he'd be at least as big as my alpha. I certainly refused to consider the possibility that I might also lose any of the men with me.

That's not happening. Please, Great Mother. Help me protect us all.

Night had fallen so quickly. I wasn't ready. Cold chills raced down my spine, yet my palms were sweaty.

"Tonight's the winter solstice," Eztli said. "The longest night of the year. You couldn't have chosen a more perfect time to call the god of darkness from his eternal sleep."

That scared me more than anything. All my careful plans and research had done nothing to bring me here. It had been a chance interview on the local news station in a crappy hotel that had brought me to this lake—with no island—in the middle of Texas.

Some unknown force had drawn me here. Coatlicue, or the god himself? Why now, after so long?

Could this truly be the mythical site of Aztlán? I stared down at the wooden case on my lap. There was only one way to know for certain. I had to use the mirror, even though I dreaded it with every fiber of my being.

"Should I start here?" I hated that my voice trembled, but I was so scared. Not for myself, but for him. For all of my Blood. "Or wait until we're closer to the water?"

Eztli closed his big, warm hand over mine, and I clutched him so hard it hurt my fingers. He didn't even flinch. As always, he was my rock. "It's up to you, my queen. If you start here, at least you're hidden from prying eyes and sheltered in the vehicle. But we may need to move to another location that we can't navigate to with the Jeep. If we end up on foot, and the mirror incapacitates you in any way, I'll carry you."

I took a deep breath and let it out slowly. Grandmama would say that I should trust my instincts. I refused to let fear dictate my decisions.

While I liked being safe and secure inside the Jeep, I would probably need to be near the water. All the accounts I'd read mentioned an island, which didn't exist anywhere in this lake. Maybe it would magically appear when I used the mirror. I might as well move closer, even though that would leave us exposed. "Let's move to the water's edge first."

Eztli nodded and immediately started giving orders. *:Diego, Luis, shift and search the area for any signs of thralls or lingering humans. Maxtla, with us.:*

Before I could move, Maxtla opened my door and offered his hand. "My queen. I'll carry the mirror, if you'd like."

I handed the case to him as I got out of the vehicle.

Flanked by Maxtla and Eztli, I tucked an arm into each of theirs as we walked into the woods.

The evening air was crisp and cool without being too cold. As we walked deeper into the forest, the freeway noises were replaced by the soft murmur of leaves in the breeze. The trees weren't familiar to me, though I recognized them as a mix of several species of pine and oak. Despite being a park dedicated to nature, something felt off. The land felt... sterile, as if it wasn't alive at all, despite the trees surrounding me.

When I walked the land at home, even outside of the nest, I felt the plants' living energy pulsing all around me. Here, the plants might as well have been made out of cardboard. I plucked a small branch off a prickly conifer to be sure it was real. Mexican pines grew in the mountains, but not anywhere near the nest. They smelled nice and spicy. I paused for a moment and pulled a few smaller branches off.

Without my request, Eztli offered a small canvas bag that I often carried out into the fields when I went scavenging for medicinal plants and herbs for Grandmama. I was surprised he'd even thought to bring it with us on the trip.

One corner of his mouth quirked. "You're a land healer at heart, my queen. You always like to take some samples home."

True. At home, I would have carried a whole sack of samples back to Grandmama's hut. I hadn't expected to have the time to collect any on this trip.

Honestly, I was procrastinating. It was like my brain wanted to focus on anything other than the task at hand. Sighing, I gave the bag back to Eztli and walked with determination along the path. Samples were well and good, but I had too much to do tonight to dawdle.

I didn't see my other two jaguars, but I could feel them

slipping through the trees ahead of us. Diego had used his special ability to leap ahead to the water's edge and was scouting the shoreline, while Luis searched the woods for anything out of the ordinary. *:The woods are empty, alpha,:* he said in our bonds. *:Not even a bunny so far.:*

:Good,: Eztli replied. *:Join Diego on the beach and find a good spot for our queen to sit.:*

After a few minutes, we broke through the trees. The shoreline was rocky, and I had to pay attention to where I stepped to avoid twisting an ankle. A gleam of light startled me for a moment, until I realized my Blood had started a small fire. Previous campers had pulled up some large logs and rocks to form a makeshift sitting area.

The crackle and gleam of the fire made me feel warm and safe. Fire would help repel thralls and other creatures. My Blood would usually see to any such threats, but if we were all involved in trying to subdue the jaguar god...

The last thing we needed was a pack of thralls to fall upon us, too.

Besides, fire was meditative and relaxing. If I needed help clearing my mind or focusing on the mirror, staring into the flames might help.

I sat on one of the logs closest to the fire, and Maxtla held out the case for me. My fingers trembled as I flipped open the latch and lifted the lid. The white cloth gleamed in the darkness. A trick of flickering firelight made it seem as if the embroidered god danced in place. Steeling myself, I pushed the cloth aside and lifted out the obsidian mirror.

I'd forgotten how heavy it was. It was an inch thick and wide enough that with my thumbs touching and fingers spread, I could barely touch the edges. Gingerly, I laid the mirror on my lap. Even though I hadn't activated it yet, I still didn't want to look directly into it. Instead, I stared out over the water, listening to the night sounds. No boats, no people, just the quiet lap of water against the rocks. An owl hooted further down the shoreline, echoing across the water.

Eztli crouched down in front of me, but to my left so I could still see the fire. Maxtla took up position behind me, so I could feel his heat against my back. Luis and Diego joined us, still in their jaguar forms. Luis stretched out on the log beside me, and Diego hopped up on a large boulder that overlooked the little makeshift camp.

They were prepared for any threat, but *I* wasn't ready. I didn't feel centered. This place was beautiful, but it wasn't mine. The land and plants didn't respond to me. "Can you take off my shoes and socks? If I can touch the ground with my bare feet, I think I'll feel more centered."

"Of course." Eztli immediately slipped off my shoes and socks.

I wriggled my toes into the sandy pebbles, soaking in the cool textures against my skin. Something deep within the earth stirred, like a monstrous dinosaur slowly lifting its head or twitching its tail. Slumberous energy pulsed beneath my feet as the land began to respond to me.

Yes. I pulled out a piece of the tree I'd picked earlier and crushed the needles in my hand, breathing in their spicy scent. I even touched one of the green needles to my tongue, tasting the sharp bite of pine.

Closing my eyes, I allowed my magic to bubble up from within me like a crystal-clear spring. This land was sick and weak, but it was starting to respond to me. No one had cared for it in centuries. It'd been paved in concrete and trod upon by millions of human feet, without a single gift of energy back into the land that made their lives possible. This wasn't my land to nurture, but it made me mourn for what we had lost. So few queens remained, and even fewer had the kind of land connection that I carried. If we lost House Zaniyah, would any other healer be able to step into my shoes and nurture our lands? Or would the forests and fields wither with disease and die?

I knew the answer. Earth would lose this magic and the land itself would die along with it. Forests would become barren wastelands, fields blasted into deserts, and even parks like this would be useless.

The only reason I was here now was a severe drought that was slowly drying up even the largest lakes across the state.

My magic would help, at least somewhat, but if I died... If I never had a child to continue our line, I feared for what our world would become.

I opened my eyes and stared into the shining black circle on my lap. Firelight glinted on the surface, but there wasn't any moonlight to brighten the it.

"It's time," I whispered softly, looking at each of my Blood. "I don't know what will happen when I activate the mirror. I don't know how Aztlán will be revealed, let alone Tezcatlipoca. But I do know one thing. I love you all."

Each of them said, "I love you, my queen."

Eztli touched my knee lightly as he shifted to his mighty jaguar. *:I love you more than life itself. You will take your jaguar god tonight.:*

I lifted my trembling left hand to his mouth, and he carefully punctured my index finger with one of his canines. Not too much blood, at least not yet. I had no idea how much I'd have to bleed before this was over.

THE FIRST DROP of my blood splattered on the glossy black surface of the mirror.

I held my breath, waiting for something to happen.

Maybe the earth would crack open. Trees would sway in a sudden hurricane. Rushing waters would reveal a magical island. Something. Surely.

I continued staring into the mirror. Waiting. My heartbeat thundered in my ears.

From a distance, I heard a jaguar roar. It sounded like Eztli, but it was so far away. Disoriented, I looked up, but he wasn't there. Everything was gone. An enormous fog bank had rolled in, wiping away the world.

My stomach quivered uneasily, but I made myself look back into the mirror. I stared back at my reflection, suddenly painfully clear despite the murky fog.

My eyes were huge, wide with fear and glistening with tears. My lips trembled. Blood dribbled from my bottom lip. I swiped at my lip and chin, afraid too much blood would drop onto the mirror, but the blood didn't smear at all in the reflection.

I looked at my fingers, and there wasn't any blood on them. I ran my tongue over my teeth, and my fangs hadn't descended.

My stomach churned harder, my breathing a short, quick pant.

I couldn't hear anything, not even the gentle lapping of the water. I inhaled deeply, but I couldn't smell my jaguars, either.

Had I already been sucked into the mirror? Was I lost to my Blood and my family?

I searched my reflection, trying to see anything on the other side that might be a clue. Firelight flickered around my image in the mirror.

It was too late. I was already doomed to Tezcatlipoca's domain, and I hadn't even seen him yet.

I looked back into my own eyes in the mirror. My mouth

moved on the other side, and though I couldn't hear the words, I knew what I said, because the words echoed in my head.

It's too late. It's over.

A surge of anger made me narrow my eyes, though my reflection didn't change. The fuck it was too late. I wasn't giving up yet. Not by a long shot.

I looked around me, trying to see through the murk. Fog swirled and flowed around me, almost like I was in an airplane flying through a cloud bank. "Help!"

At least I could hear my own voice. That was something, wasn't it?

"Tezcatlipoca, Smoking Mirror, Lord of Darkness and Sorcery, I come to you in search of your jaguar aspect, Tepeyollotl."

I turned, slowly, straining to see anything through the clouds.

"I call jaguars."

Nothing but my own words echoed back at me.

What had Grandmama said about the mirror? I tried to remember her words exactly.

It would show me truths about myself, and I might not like them. People had gone mad rather than face the truths they saw staring back at them.

I looked back at myself, and yeah, the pitiful, terrified look on my face infuriated me. I knew I was stronger than that. I had searched the world for twenty years to find the mythical Aztlán. I had called four jaguar Blood. I had carefully honed my power, year after year. I'd built my nest's defenses to better protect my child, if only I could have her. Not even the queen of New York City had been able to break through yet, and she was the most powerful queen in the Americas.

I had the nerve to search out one of the most feared and respected Aztec gods, with the presumptuous hope that he'd be willing to sire my child. That he'd be willing to fuck an Aima queen, when he had likely spent an eternity working his way through the Aztec goddesses of Aztlán.

What hope did I have of calling him to my side? Let alone convincing him to sire my child?

Confusion flickered through me. Was I weak and scared? Or was I arrogant beyond belief?

Staring at myself in the mirror, I had to admit that I was both. I *was* terrified. I wasn't a strong queen by any stretch, and though I was stronger now than when Grandmama had first passed the Zaniyah queendom to me, I was still only a minor queen. I always would be, even if I managed to have a daughter.

Even so, I was determined to do everything in my power, even attempt to bend a god to my will, in order to have her.

My power wasn't earthshattering, but I'd always felt fulfilled and grateful for the blessings Coatlicue had granted me. I loved being able to heal people. I enjoyed caring for my lands. I loved touching a seed and giving it an extra little push with my power, willing it to grow strong, and then watching it do exactly that.

As I willed.

I focused on my image again, determined to drive the fear out of my eyes. *You are stronger than this. You are strong enough. For anything.*

The Mayte on the other side lifted her chin slightly. Her eyes narrowed. She licked the blood from her lip.

Yes. It's working.

I tipped my face up to the swirling sky and shouted, "Tez-catlipoca! I need your help, Great Lord of Darkness. Lord of the Night, please come to my aid!"

I checked the reflection to see if anything had changed.

The other Mayte smiled at me and her mouth moved again. *Thank you.*

Then she turned away, and all I saw where my reflection had been was a black, empty hole.

9

EZTLI

I'd accepted the fact that I might die on this expedition. In fact, it was likely, as far as I was concerned. I wouldn't give up my position by my queen's side, let alone in her heart, easily. If the jaguar god wanted to have her, he would have to go through me first.

But my very worst nightmare was now unfolding before me. My queen looked up from the mirror, but it wasn't her. Her eyes were completely black. She didn't know me. She didn't even know herself.

"Mayte? My queen?"

Ignoring me, she stood and walked into the water.

I plunged after her and seized her arm, but I couldn't seem to hold on to her. She wasn't fighting or resisting me— my hands simply slid off her. I couldn't stop her. She walked deeper and deeper into the water, and I could only watch in horror as the water inched up to her neck. Then to her chin.

She's going to drown. Just like her mother.

No. I couldn't bear to lose her. If anyone had to die tonight, it should be me. I had already envisioned it countless times. I would gladly die so she could have her heart's desire.

I could already see her smiling down at a baby girl, a tiny mirror image of her mother.

Her head sank beneath the water and I roared with fury. I grabbed for her again and touched her. I felt her skin against my fingers, but my grip wouldn't hold. I couldn't pull her back to me, to safety, no matter how hard I tried. Her hair swirled in the water, sweeping over my fingers one last time. Then she was gone.

I dived into the water, straining to see even a glimpse of her skin. I had to find her. My queen. My heart. My soul. If I lost her...

Something slammed into me like a freight train. I stared up at a night sky glittering with thousands of diamonds. But I couldn't breathe. My chest felt like it'd been caved in by a heavy weight.

No, that was merely my empty ribcage. My heart was gone. Dead. With my queen.

"You would die for her?" The low voice came from nowhere. Everywhere.

I strained to move. To even breathe. I had to get up. I had to find her. Drag her out of the water. She was an Aima queen. *My* queen. It wasn't too late to save her.

But all I managed to do was tip my chin down slightly. A massive dark shape sat on top of my chest. No wonder I couldn't breathe.

The shape moved, lowering its heavy head down toward me. Jaguar. The biggest fucking cat I'd ever seen in my life. I was alpha, but this cat was...

God.

His coat was jet black and as shiny as the obsidian mirror. Instead of large golden eyes, he had two black eyes that reflected my own image back at me. I could see myself in his eyes. The stunned look on my face. Lines of grief etched around my eyes and mouth. The tears shining in my eyes. I couldn't bear to live without my queen. Better that I died, and she lived, happy with this god she'd managed to call, than for me to live a single moment without her.

"Interesting," the giant jaguar said. Then as casually as if he were a house cat, he stepped down off me, and went to sniff her other jaguars.

I pushed to my feet and wavered a moment, my head spinning. My queen. I had to find her.

"Sit," the jaguar growled, not even looking at me, though I felt his command roll through my body like an earthquake.

I sat. Hard. On the ground, right where I'd been standing.

I might be alpha, but he was the jaguar god, and my beast didn't hesitate to obey him. I didn't even remember shifting back to my human form.

"Think, *alpha*," he said mockingly. "Remember exactly what you saw. What is real? What is only a vision?"

I jerked my gaze away from the lake and looked back to where my queen had been sitting. She still sat on the log, staring intently into the obsidian mirror on her lap.

When her head sank beneath the water, her hair had been loose, even though I had braided her hair with my own hands this morning. The whole thing had been a vision. Now I couldn't breathe because of relief, not agony.

The black jaguar sat on his haunches and watched her, his tail flicking back and forth. He watched her so intently that the hairs on my nape prickled. Other than his tail, he didn't move, but he was poised, ready to pounce. To feast? To rip her to shreds? I had no idea.

"What are you waiting for?" I asked hesitantly.

He didn't look away from her. "To see if she lives or dies."

MAYTE

I stared at the empty mirror, my mind shaken. What did it mean? Was I dead? Would I be trapped here in this gray nothingness forever?

"What is your name?" A deep voice rumbled through the fog.

Shivering, I clutched the mirror harder and willed my voice not to falter. "Mayte Zaniyah."

"You have passed the first test, Mayte Zaniyah."

I didn't know whether to feel relieved that I'd passed—or sick with dread at the thought of more tests. I didn't know how much more my mind could take.

I'd never been so alone. So lost. It was a terrible feeling.

Even growing up without my mother or father, I'd had Grandmama. I'd had my twin brothers. There were countless people in our nest that I'd seen every single day. I couldn't recall a time where I'd been as alone as I was in this moment, surrounded by endless gray fog. My mind kept searching for something recognizable, like a landmark, or at least a color. Something other than the fog swirling from nowhere.

"You called me, Mayte Zaniyah. What do you want?"

Tezcatlipoca. I'd done it. I'd managed to call him from his resting place. I gulped with nerves, frantically searching the fog. Where was he? What did he look like? What would he do to me?

"Well? I grow impatient, queen."

At least he knew what I was, though I thought I detected a bit of sarcasm in his voice, as if his lip had curled with disdain. "I want a child. A daughter. To carry on the Zaniyah line."

A rough sound echoed through the fog. At first, my nerves shrilled with terror, but then I realized he was laughing.

And that pissed me off.

"I've looked for you for twenty years."

He grunted with disgust. "You *looked* with your eyes. You made your plans and plotted your maps and wasted twenty years looking for a fairytale. You didn't look with your heart. You didn't look with your blood. Because you knew if you looked with magic, you would find what you sought immediately. Aztlán isn't a place on a map. It's not at this lake you've searched for so diligently. Aztlán is accessed through the mirror. Through yourself. You could have touched Aztlán at any time once you had the mirror at your disposal."

Blinking rapidly, I hunched my shoulders, my arms curling over my chest as if he'd struck me. I couldn't breathe.

He'd wounded me, definitely, but only with the truth.

"I'm a coward," I whispered, brushing tears away.

The mirror suddenly lit up, drawing my gaze to the image unfolding. I stared at my bedroom at home. My bed, covered with the quilt Grandmama had made for me ages ago. Eztli strode into the room, carrying me. He tossed me onto the bed, and I squealed with laughter. It made me smile, my eyes filling with happy tears.

"You were given much to love. Yet you never embraced it fully."

I wasn't sure what Tezcatlipoca meant, until the image blurred, and I was in the hotel bed with all four of my Blood. My cheeks heated at the raw sexuality. The mirror confronted me with *my* desire.

But they touched me differently this time. Eztli didn't seduce me with a slow, gentle massage.

He had his hand fisted in my hair so tightly that my scalp screamed with sensation, my head pinned back against him.

Luis and Diego didn't carefully suck on my nipples. They bit. They tugged. It hurt.

Even here, on the smoky side of the mirror, I felt that pain throb through my breasts, shooting fiery streams of lust straight down to my pussy.

I swallowed hard, fighting down the lust. That wasn't me. Was it? Shame squeezed my throat shut. I averted my face, refusing to look at the image any longer, though I could feel the dampness between my thighs. I ached with need. To be touched.

To be hurt.

Tezcatlipoca let out a rumbling growl that made the hairs on my arms stand up. My heart thudded and skipped with terror. I had never heard a wild jaguar make that sound before, but I recognized it for what it was.

A warning that my time was up. He was going to kill me.

I had failed the test.

I made myself look back at the mirror, hoping that would quell his anger, but the mirror had gone black again.

Fur brushed my arm, making me twitch with surprise. I jerked my head around, but he wasn't there. I could smell him, though. Jaguar, mixed with the pungent smell of burning copal incense. I couldn't quite place all the different resins that had been used in that incense. Everyone's blend of tree resins was slightly different. Grandmama's always smelled slightly of lemon, but his scent smelled more like smoking chocolate and coffee.

Something sharp grazed my arm and I recoiled, my hand clamping over the spot automatically. Thick blood welled between my fingers.

"Wait," I gasped. "I still want to try. I want to know the truth."

I felt the moist, hot blast of his breath against my nape. Shivering, I held firm. I wouldn't run away. I wouldn't scream. Even if he bit my spine in half.

"Why would a queen descended from the Mother of the Gods feel shame at anything in her heart? That is what I want to know, Mayte Zaniyah." He paused a moment and gripped the back of my neck in his mighty jaws. I could feel every vicious tooth scratching my skin. A fraction more pressure from his jaws, and he would tear my head off. "I want to know why you only allowed one of your jaguars to love you at a time. Why you hide, even from the alpha who would die to save you. Why would you deny him anything? Especially the truth?"

His words cut worse than his claws and teeth. He was right. I hid, even from Eztli. My alpha. I loved him. We'd made love countless times, but somehow, I had always managed to hold back one small piece of myself.

One small, devastating truth.

"I'm a queen," I whispered, my throat shredding as if I'd swallowed sharp shards of obsidian. "Queens are fearless. Strong. Protective. They wield their magic to protect their people. Queens take what they want. What they need. They don't…" I swallowed, wincing at the sour, bitter taste of fear on my tongue. "They aren't weak. They aren't afraid. They don't need to be hurt, even with love. They certainly don't submit. Ever."

"Who says these lies?" Tezcatlipoca whispered, dragging his canines back and forth over the bumps of my spine.

"Me." My teeth chattered, and I clutched the mirror so hard my fingers ached. "I say these lies. To myself."

"Use this truth, queen, and take your jaguar god. If you dare."

He sank his teeth into my spine, and the mirror shattered into a thousand pieces.

10

MAYTE

Someone was screaming. Me. I fell through endless black. I couldn't see anything, but I felt wind rushing past me. I smelled blood. My blood.

I thrashed and flailed, trying to slow my descent. I didn't want to die. Not yet. I had too much to do. I had to tell Eztli…

I slammed into my body so hard that my scream cut off with a startled gasp. My eyes flew open, my chest heaving. I sucked in a deep breath and screamed again. I clamped my hand over the back of my neck, hoping to stem the blood flow from Tezcatlipoca's bite. I had never tried to heal myself. I wasn't sure that I could, especially not a wound dealt by a god.

There wasn't any blood pouring from gashes or punctures. I could move my arm. My spine wasn't snapped in half.

But the largest jaguar I'd ever seen in my life crouched before me.

As soon as I looked into his mirrored eyes, he pounced.

Instinctively, I slung my arms up over my face, but he

didn't go for my throat. He seized my braid in his jaws and started dragging me down to the shoreline, like a jaguar would drag his kill.

My Blood roared immediately and attacked. Eztli's beast leapt onto the black jaguar's broad back and dug in with all four paws. But he looked like a stuffed toy on top of the mighty god. My alpha, who dwarfed my other Blood and made wild jaguars look like household kitties.

I thumped my fists into the black jaguar's face, trying to find his eyes, but he ignored me as if I was as inconsequential as a gnat. Cold water splashed me in the face as he started wading into the lake.

He was taking me away, through a portal to the other-world, as my mother had tried to do to reach her lover.

No. I won't leave so easily.

Water closed over my head, but I was an Aima queen. I didn't need to breathe.

I needed to feed.

I grabbed his shoulders and hauled myself closer to the jaguar god. Sinking my fangs into his chest, I punctured his hide easily. His blood filled my mouth, along with his fur.

A god's blood.

He tasted like he smelled—copal incense, blended with smoking chocolate and coffee, as if the ripened fruits had been left out in the noon sun to dry, and then someone had lit them on fire.

Through my bonds, I felt my Blood attack. They bit and tore and shredded the mighty god, trying to force him to release me. Trying to save me.

:Stop!: I shouted through all of my bonds, even the freshly-forged bond with the god who was dragging me into the lake.

Miracle of miracles, he did exactly as I commanded.

Eztli

DRIPPING wet and coughing up water, my queen clung to the black jaguar's throat. His blood ran from her mouth, as well as from dozens of minor wounds we'd given him. Not that they'd slowed him down in the slightest.

"Take me back to the fire."

Still holding her by her braid, the big cat turned and hauled her back toward the campfire we'd lit on the beach.

My queen. Dragged like a rag doll over rocks and sand. Rage bubbled up inside me, but what could I do? Tepeyollotl was *the* jaguar god. He'd already proven exactly how much power he wielded over me.

He sat back on his haunches by the fire but didn't release her braid. His claim on her was clear, though he did obey her commands. So why didn't she tell him to release her?

Worry crawled through my veins like angry ants. I couldn't help remembering the way she'd looked at me in the vision, as if she wasn't herself any longer. Had the mirror corrupted her somehow? Changed her personality? Was she possessed by Tezcatlipoca?

Sagging against the big cat's chest, she dangled in his grasp. But her voice didn't quiver with fear when she said. "Shift. All of you."

We did as she commanded, and I watched, curious, as Tepeyollotl was revealed in his human form. I wasn't surprised that he was a big man with a broad, barrel chest, thick arms and thighs, and long black hair that hung in thick, twisted cables almost to his waist. His skin was darker than mine, only slightly lighter than the obsidian mirror or his beast. He might be the size of a sumo wrestler, but otherwise, he looked…

Normal.

Like a man. The same as me.

Then I noticed he still gripped her braid, only this time in his right hand. He kept her head under his control.

I dragged my gaze from his powerful hand locked in my queen's hair to her eyes, staring back at me. Tremulous. Scared, now, in a way that she hadn't been before.

"I saw myself in the mirror," she finally whispered, her eyes pleading with me to understand. To forgive.

For what?

Confused, I could only nod, immediately, as I moved closer to her. I would forgive anything. It didn't matter to me, not as long as she was safe.

She dropped her gaze to her hands, gripped together tightly in front of her. "I didn't know."

Tepeyollotl gave a sharp tug on her hair that made her gasp, her entire body jolting with shock.

"I suspected," she said quickly. "I hid it. Even from myself. I was ashamed."

I shot a hard look at the man abusing her hair. Let him strike me down if he liked, but I wouldn't back down. He'd have to kill me if he thought to hurt her. I took her trembling hands between both of mine and rubbed them lightly, trying to ease some of her fear. "My queen should never be ashamed. I don't care what you hid. It doesn't matter to me."

"That's why…" Her voice broke and tears dripped onto my hand, alarming me even more. She took a ragged breath and tried again. "That's why I only ever took you one at a time. I was afraid I wouldn't be able to hide it if you were all touching me. Surely one of you would discover the truth, and I didn't… I was afraid…"

"Mayte," I ground out harshly. "Nothing you could ever do or say would change our love. You're our queen. Always. Why would you hide anything from us?"

"I didn't want you to think I was weak. Or regret swearing your life to me."

"Never," I retorted fiercely, squeezing her hands hard in mine. Tepeyollotl growled softly, probably a warning, but fuck the jaguar god if he thought I would meekly allow her to believe that I would ever surrender my queen's love.

She lifted her gaze to mine, and the fragile look in her eyes tore my heart from my chest. She wasn't afraid or hurt. She wasn't angry at me for squeezing her hands. And she still didn't order the jaguar god to release her hair.

Because she *liked* the way he pinned her against him.

Relieved, I almost laughed, but I was afraid she'd mistake my reaction for ridicule. Instead, I squeezed her hands harder and lifted them both toward my mouth. I pried her clenched fists open, so I could plant a kiss on each palm, deliberately using my larger hands and strength to force her fingers open. "Did you honestly think that I didn't know?"

Her mouth fell open with surprise, and this time I did laugh, though I dragged her into my arms, at least as far as Tepeyollotl's unrelenting grip on her hair allowed. "I know every beat of your heart, my love, but I would never force you into any situation. I felt your unease. As alpha, perhaps I should have pushed you harder to face that discomfort, but I thought to let you come to the conclusion in your own time. As you've done."

She buried her face against my throat. "You're not disappointed? I'm not a strong queen, Eztli. I never will be. And now…"

This time, when Tepeyollotl jerked on her hair, I approved. I released her, and he dragged her back against him. "You're gravely mistaken. A strong queen knows what she wants, what she needs, and she takes it, no matter what it is."

Tepeyollotl twisted her around by her hair, forcing her to

look into his gleaming eyes that glittered like the obsidian mirror, rippling with power. "If you want to take *me*, Mayte Zaniyah, then you'll ask me for exactly what you want, as the strong woman you are."

S haking, I stared up into the god's dark, shining eyes. I had his blood burning inside me. If he chose, he could certainly rip us all to shreds and disappear back into Aztlán.

But he stayed. Waiting for me to decide if I would take what I most wanted in the world. Even if it meant I had to surrender my pride and embrace all that I was, inside and out. No matter how uncomfortable it made me.

Already, my body hummed with unexpected pleasure. The tugs on my hair. The force Eztli had used to squeeze my hands. Such powerful, strong men, willing to do anything I asked.

But I had to *ask*.

I'd thought I wanted a child more than anything in the world. Enough to risk my life, my nest, even my beloved Blood, all to sire a daughter to continue the Zaniyah line. And I did still want this child. Desperately.

But whether I had a daughter or not, I would never be complete if I didn't accept that beneath my power and magic,

I ached for a lover's strong, unforgiving hand. I burned to be taken. Hard. Out of control. Even hurt.

Like when I'd called a centuries-old Blood, who'd never had his own queen, to my bed the very first time.

"Please," I whispered.

Tepeyollotl twisted his wrist, wrapping my hair tighter around his fist. "Please what?"

I moaned, helpless to hold back the small sound. "Hurt me. While you make love to me."

He turned his attention to Eztli. For a moment, I froze, afraid that I'd offended or upset my alpha, but when I touched his bond, all I felt was a river of molten lava.

"What does her alpha say to this request?"

Eztli's voice rumbled with the growl of his beast. "I would beg only that I be allowed to love her, too."

"Granted," Tepeyollotl agreed. "Remove these wet clothes. Our queen is cold." He looked to my other Blood one by one. "Are you willing to participate if called upon?"

"Nothing will keep me from our queen," Maxtla said. "Not even you."

"Agreed," Luis and Diego replied together.

Tepeyollotl laughed softly and focused back on me. "So eager. So willing to please you in any way you wish, even if I bat them away like annoying cubs. It's a shame that you waited so long to fully take these young jaguars."

Maxtla grumped beneath his breath. "Nine hundred isn't exactly young."

"It is for someone who remembers a time before humans roamed this earth." Tepeyollotl narrowed his eyes on the man behind me. "She shivers."

The sound of my clothing shredding away made me shiver harder, but not because I was cold. Eztli used his claws to tear my hoodie and jeans away from my body. The sound of ripping material was barbaric. Feral.

It made my blood simmer hotter in my veins.

Tepeyollotl pulled me upright so I stood before him, naked and exposed. Had it just been last night that I was so embarrassed by all my Blood looking at me? Seeing me vulnerable? Aching with need? It seemed so long ago.

He took his time looking at me, even making me turn around and face Eztli. Then Maxtla. Diego. Luis. The god waited for me to look into each of my Blood's eyes, acknowledge my need, and see that nothing had changed.

My Blood still looked at me as their queen, whom they loved more than anything in this world. Nothing would ever change that.

Even if I asked the god of jaguars to hurt me. Especially if I asked it of them, too.

Tepeyollotl jerked me back around to face him. I wasn't sure why, not at first. He didn't make any demands of me, but merely stared back at me steadily. I allowed my gaze to run over his body. He sat on the ground, leaning back against the log I'd sat on earlier, yet his head was barely below mine. He was a big man. A strong man.

I dropped my eyes lower and gulped. A *very* big man.

Then it dawned on me. The god of jaguars was erect. He wanted *me*.

"Prepare her, alpha."

Eztli engulfed me with his body and heat, eagerly taking me down to my knees on the ground. He thrust into me so hard that I fell forward and had to grab onto Tepeyollotl's massive thighs on either side of me to brace myself. Eztli had made love to me many times over the years, but he'd never felt so large inside me before, nor as out of control.

He was as aroused as Tepeyollotl. My admission had not put a dent in Eztli's desire at all. Instead, it had inflamed him more than ever.

His arms slid around me so he could cup my breasts. His

fingers sought my nipples, as he'd done last night, but this time, he pinched. Hard.

I moaned deep in my throat. He always felt incredible inside of me, but the small pain made my nerves scream with sensation. I twitched around his cock, already coming. I would have let my head fall back against his shoulder if I could have, but Tepeyollotl refused to surrender my braid. In fact, he tugged me closer to him, bringing me eye-level with his magnificent cock.

As an Aima queen, putting a man's dick in my mouth wasn't something I ever considered, for fear my fangs would cause him too much damage. Eztli would have allowed me to do so, without question, but I'd never wanted to risk hurting him. Not like that.

Tepeyollotl released my braid, and yeah, for a moment, disappointment rippled through me. Until his palm slid around my nape and he squeezed so hard I moaned again, making him chuckle with a dark, sexual heat that turned my moan into a whimper.

"That's better," he said a silky voice that somehow managed to convey both menace and lust. "You want more than pain, little queen. You want to surrender, too. What should I make her do, alpha?"

Eztli bit my earlobe, making me jolt against him. "You should make her suck your dick while I feed."

"An excellent idea."

His hand was so heavy on my neck. So strong. It snapped something inside me. Something that I'd shoved away and locked deep inside me. That lock sprang open as he hauled my mouth onto his dick. He didn't bring me gently to him. He didn't care about my fangs. I had a feeling he wouldn't have cared if I deliberately tried to bite him, though that was the furthest thing from my mind.

The locked doors inside me swung open wider. All the

chains and locks and secrets I thought I'd buried so well were exposed. Tepeyollotl pushed into my mouth so deeply that I couldn't breathe. Relentless, he filled me, making me choke. Breaking me apart.

No, that was Eztli, sinking his fangs into my throat.

I hung, suspended between them, consumed with complete and utter ecstasy. I'd never known such freedom. Such relief. I didn't hold anything back. I moaned around Tepeyollotl's cock. I clenched harder on Eztli's inside me. My blood danced and sang in my veins, filled to the brim with power. It welled up inside me like a geyser.

I had never felt so much power.

Eztli shuddered on top of me, his release pushing me higher. The only thing that kept me from soaring into the night sky was Tepeyollotl's heavy hand on the back of my head.

He pulled me up onto his lap, shifting me onto his thighs. "Take me at your speed, little queen."

I sank onto his cock slowly. Loudly. Because I couldn't help the raw sounds of desire escaping my throat. He was so big, everywhere, not just his cock. One big hand palmed my head easily. His other hand roamed my body, plucking and playing me like a delicate harp. Small pains blended with the pleasure, until I honestly couldn't tell the difference. It was wondrous.

He was wondrous.

This was wondrous.

Why had I been so terrified of my secret need? When I could have felt so… free?

I didn't have to control my reactions or worry about showing too much. I had already given them everything. They knew everything. And they were still here. Loving me.

When I had him seated deeply inside me, Tepeyollotl gave a deep grunt of satisfaction. "So good. I had forgotten the incredible pleasures to be found in the flesh. What else may I give you, little queen?"

"You can feed from me."

"You would take Mountain Heart, the jaguar god, as Blood?"

For a moment, I was afraid I'd offended him, but he laughed roughly and nudged his hips upward, sliding even deeper into me. I twitched and jerked in his arms as if he'd electrocuted me.

"Very well. I've never been Blood before. What else, my queen?"

I fisted my hands in the heavy cords of his hair on either side of his face, and he obligingly lowered his head so I could touch my lips to his. "I liked little queen."

"Ask," he rumbled against my lips. "So I may fulfill my little queen's every desire."

"Can you give me a daughter, Mountain Heart?"

"Yes. On one condition."

I pulled back enough to look into his eyes. I stared back at myself, mirrored in his gaze. But this time, I knew who I was, what I wanted most of all, and I wasn't ashamed of that truth any longer.

"If I must call you my little queen, and he is your alpha, then you must call me your heart."

Tears burned my eyes. He stated his intentions so clearly. I could keep Eztli. He would always be my alpha. Tepeyollotl would bend to my wishes, even as he gave me the strength and control I had secretly desired. And, of course, he would give me the child I so desperately needed to continue the Zaniyah line.

All I had to do was love him, too.

No more hiding. No more secrets. No more fruitless external searches, when the truth I needed had been hidden inside me all along. I stared up at him, proudly, my eyes shining as brightly as his. "My heart, please make me yours for all time."

He turned my head to the side, baring my throat. And this time, when he bit me, I screamed with pleasure, not terror.

The End

READ the rest of the Their Vampire Queen series, starting with Queen Takes Knights.

PRINCESS TAKES UNICORNS

A bonus chapter written for the Triune. More to come!

"Wake, child," a woman whispered. "I have something to show you."

I sat up, rubbing my eyes. She sounded so familiar, but when I looked at her face, I didn't know her. Fear squeezed my throat and I cowered back against my pillows, hugging myself. How did she get inside the nest? A stranger? "Who are you?"

My arms still had light, white scratches from the giant bird's talons. Mama frowned every time she saw them, because we were supposed to heal really fast. The scratches hadn't been that deep, but they had still left scars.

Something told me if this woman scratched me...

I wouldn't see Mama ever again.

The stranger had long shiny black hair, and her eyes made my chest feel like I couldn't breathe. Her eyes saw everything. It felt like she unzipped my stomach and rummaged around inside, looking for something she'd lost.

"My name is Isis." Her voice was so gentle despite her eyes. "Do you know me?"

I hadn't heard of Isis, until our queen came and made Mama her sib. Isis was Queen Shara's goddess, like Coatlicue was mine, Mama's, and Grandmama's.

A goddess. Sitting on the edge of my bed. Talking to me like I was her friend. I gulped and nodded. "You're our pretty queen's goddess."

She smiled. "Yes, Shara's very pretty, but so are you. You're also as brave as she is, did you know that? You escaped the sun god."

I looked away, tears burning my eyes. I hadn't felt very brave when the giant bird had swooped down out of the sky and carried me away. I sniffed and wiped my nose. "He killed Esperanza. He almost ate me. I wasn't brave. I cried a lot."

"Crying doesn't mean you weren't brave."

"I was scared," I whispered, shivering.

"It's okay to be scared, too. You were still very brave. You still fought. That's all that matters. You didn't give up. That's why I thought you might be able to help me."

I dared a quick look back into Her eyes. "Me? Help you?"

"Yes, if you're willing. May I show you something?"

I nodded, and She held her hand out. I took it and before I could slide out of bed, we were standing outside in front of the huge tree Shara had grown. I'd never seen anything like it before. It was so tall and wide it looked old, even older than Grandmama, but the queen had grown it from nothing in a single night. Mama hadn't let me stay to watch, but I heard the whispers.

Shara had grown the tree from blood. Lots of blood. A queen's sacrifice.

Someday, I would be queen. I'd need to be able to make sacrifices like that, too. I didn't know if I could do it.

Thinking about it made my tummy feel like I'd eaten too much cake.

I probably had eaten too many sweets. Sarah had been making cake every day because I was sure that cake would make my unicorns come to me quicker. Papa had said so.

"I'm going to show you a secret." Isis smiled at me. "Ready?"

She stepped into the deep, dark crack inside the tree. She didn't pull me in after Her, but paused, looking back at me and letting me decide if I wanted to follow.

The hole was yucky. There might be spiders. I hated spiders. Uncle Itztli hated spiders, too.

But I didn't want to let a goddess down. I wanted to be brave. Like Shara. Like Her.

"We'll only be gone a few minutes," Isis said. "I promise to see you home safely and back in your bed by morning."

I took a deep breath and stepped into the dark hole with Her. She held my hand firmly, which helped, though Her hand didn't feel right against mine. I couldn't figure out what it was that made Her different.

Complete darkness made my heart pound, but another step and I could see light shining through another crack. Isis ducked as we stepped out into a place that took my breath away. It was early morning. The sun peeked above the hills in the distance, but the sky was still mostly dark with streaks of pink and purple. My favorite colors.

Birds cawed and sang like nothing I'd ever heard before. Monkeys screeched in the branches above, and one even waved to us as we walked by. I could barely see over the tall grass. I'd never seen anything like this place, except maybe in one of my favorite movies. "Is this Africa?"

She gave me a secretive smile. "Yes, it is."

"Through the tree? In our yard?"

"Yes, but you must keep it a secret. Only Shara is able to

work the tree magic to travel, but since you're her heir, you can too."

Glee bubbled up in me, making me laugh. I could do something that Mama couldn't do. "Can I go see Queen Shara?"

"Anytime you wish, but make sure she's home before you go."

As we walked into the savannah, I tried to see if I could feel Shara. She'd spoken in my head before, like when the bird took me. But I couldn't talk to her. Mama wouldn't let me use the phone. If I wanted to see if Shara was home...

I needed a bond with her, like Mama's and Papa's. If they didn't mind.

Sweat ran down my face before we finally paused near another huge tree. This one didn't have a crack in its trunk and it was bushier. Something lay in the darkness beneath the branches. It made a low panting sound that made goose-bumps race down my arms despite the heat. A lion? A jaguar? Jaguars lived in Africa, I thought. Maybe I could talk to it like Mama and tell it not to eat me.

Isis ducked beneath the thick branches to approach what-ever hid in the shade. Surely even the meanest, hungriest lion wouldn't try to eat a goddess, and She'd promised I would be home before morning.

I tiptoed into the darkness beneath the tree. A dark shape lay near the trunk. I inched closer, straining my senses. Other than the heavy, labored breathing, it didn't make any other noise. It didn't smell bad like a skunk, but it definitely didn't smell like fur. It wasn't any kind of cat.

I blinked, and the shape solidified into a boy. The heavy panting disappeared. He sat with his back against the tree, his knees pulled up to his chest. He leaned forward, revealing more of his face. He wasn't that much older than me, maybe ten or twelve. His skin was black, his hair in tight braids that swept back like wings on either side of his head.

He met Isis's gaze and dared to glare at Her.

What kind of boy would glare at the Great One?

"You've come to kill me, then."

"Why would I wish any child dead?" Isis asked softly. "Let alone a child of your power. You could be of great use to us."

He looked at me, then, his eyes as wide with surprise as mine.

I let out a startled squeak. "*Us*? What can I do?"

"You can save him." She bent down between us and looked at me solemnly, Her dark eyes gleaming even in the shadows. "He's a king. Do you know what that means?"

I shook my head.

He flickered again, and the boy was replaced by a cow shape with short, stubby legs. In the darkness, it was hard to tell exactly what he was. Maybe a hippopotamus or a rhinoceros. Definitely large, heavy, and ugly. He snorted at me and I scrambled back another step, before I caught myself.

I was Xochitl Zaniyah, daughter of Coatlicue, Mother of the Gods, and heir to Shara Isador, last daughter of the Great One. She had called me Princess of Unicorns.

I tipped my chin up, determined not to be afraid, especially of this gray, ugly beast.

"He was born with the ability to shift," Isis said. "But he can't control his power. He needs a queen to help him." She met my gaze, Her eyes tugging on me again, making it hard to breathe. "He needs you."

I wanted to be brave, but my voice still quivered. "I'm not a queen yet."

She gave me a gentle smile. "You're more queen than you realize, child. He has nowhere else to go that's safe. His queen mother was forced from her sib's nest when she delivered a king, and she was killed last night. He will be a formidable Blood one day and protect you well."

"But..." I blinked rapidly, trying not to cry. "Queen Shara said I could have unicorns."

Isis nodded and looked off into the distance, as if She could see thousands of miles away. "They're coming, but not for several years yet. They must grow in power too before they can come to you. Keras needs help now, and he can protect you while you grow up together."

He flickered again back to his boy shape and dropped his head down on top of his knees. He had no nest. His mother had died. He had no one. And his beast was ugly.

He was nothing like what I'd dreamed of. Beautiful ponies like Esperanza, only all the colors of the rainbow with sweeping wings that carried them effortlessly through the sky.

Not this gray, heavy creature with funny legs. He wouldn't be able to run very fast, let alone fly.

What would I do if Mama died? If I lost our nest? At least I had our new queen.

This boy had no one.

No one but me.

I stepped closer and dropped down to my knees beside him, but before I could say anything, he growled at me. "Go away. I don't need your pity."

"What are you? I mean, what's your animal?"

"Rhinoceros."

"Oh." I tried to think of something nice to say about his beast. "You'll have a horn one day, right? That's cool."

He lifted his head, his eyes flashing in the darkness. "Of course, I'll have a horn. All male rhinos do. Most are killed for them."

"Mama calls jaguars, but I don't want cats. I don't know

what kind of shape I'll have, but our new queen can shift into a black jaguar with wings. She was so pretty."

His face tightened but he didn't look away. "Mama could shift into a rhino too, but she still died."

Such pain shone in his eyes. I shifted closer and picked up one of his hands in mine. His nails were torn and bloody, his knuckles swollen, and his palms scraped, as if he'd been in a fight. "Who killed her?"

He didn't pull away and his hand trembled in mine. "A giant crocodile. I've never seen one so big before, and it was a strange color. I tried…" He blew out a long, shaking breath. "I couldn't save her. My beast wouldn't come when I needed it. She died so I could escape."

"What color was it?"

"Light colored, almost white, but it wasn't an albino. It had yellow eyes."

I shivered. "A huge golden bird tried to drag me through a portal to Ra, but Queen Shara pulled me back out. That's why I wanted Blood that could fly."

"Even if I could have controlled my beast, I don't have a horn yet. I'm too young. I couldn't have saved Mama."

He was silent several moments. Long enough for me to listen to the bird calls and wonder what time it was at home. What Sarah might make for breakfast. I wanted to go back to the tree and see if I could find Shara's nest.

"I can't fly, but when my horn comes in, I'll stab anything that tries to steal you. Then I'll trample it into the ground," he whispered fiercely. His fingers tightened on mine, hard enough it hurt. "I'll be your Blood. I'll do what you ask. As long as you let me come back here when I'm strong and hunt down the crocodile that killed my mother."

"Okay. But I'm coming with you."

"Deal."

I looked up at Isis. "How do I make him my Blood?"

She reached out, palm up, and I slipped my hand into hers. "You give him blood and take his in turn. Then he will always be yours, and you will always be his queen."

One of Her long, painted nails made a small cut on my wrist, so quickly that I didn't even feel it. My blood welled up and She guided my wrist to the boy.

I'd tasted blood before, but I'd never given anyone mine. I held my breath, unsure what would happen. What it would feel like. He leaned toward my arm and sniffed at my wrist, making a low whuffing sound like his beast. Then he licked the trail of blood and closed his mouth over the small cut.

Goosebumps raced down my arms and my spine tingled. My hair felt like I'd rolled around on the carpet with Papa. If I touched anything, I'd probably blow my finger off.

He lifted his head and blinked slowly, as if he was waking from a dream. "My queen."

"And now it's your turn," Isis said.

He held up his arm and she made a small cut for me.

The smell of his blood made my stomach rumble like I hadn't eaten for days, but I wasn't hungry. Not exactly. He lifted his wrist up for me but didn't press the cut to my mouth. It was my choice. I liked that.

I breathed him in like he'd done to me. He smelled like the ground after a spring rain. Earthy, but also bursting with life.

If I tasted him...

I could do anything. Anything at all. Even tear apart a gigantic crocodile or golden eagle.

I pressed my mouth to the cut and tasted his blood. Mama always made me think of the jungle. Papa, like his jaguar, but sparkling with ancient magic. Queen Shara had tasted like the darkest, richest chocolate cake that Sarah made with her secret recipe.

Keras tasted like coffee beans and spices laid out to roast

in the summer sun. His thoughts fluttered into my mind like butterflies. My eyes filled with tears at his grief. His horror, watching his mother fight the crocodile, even knowing she couldn't win. She'd died. Alone. Without a single Blood to help her.

:You will always have me now,: he whispered in my head. *:You will never fight alone.:*

:Neither will you.:

Isis laid Her hand on my head, or I might have kept drinking from him for hours. He tasted that good. I might never get enough.

"Thank you for taking care of Keras. Now I would like to give you a reward."

I shook my head and grinned at him. "I have a friend now. That's reward enough for me. I don't have anyone to play with, and Papa gets tired of me trying to ride his jaguar."

She smiled but shook Her head. "No, I insist. You asked for unicorn Blood, and here I've gifted you with a fine king rhino instead. So…" She punctured Her own wrist and offered Her blood.

A goddess's blood. Given to me.

Eyes wide, I stared at her. "But… I'm not your daughter, not like Queen Shara."

"You're her heir and she's my daughter, and so you are my daughter too. I'd be honored to give you a small taste of power that should satisfy your yearning for unicorns until they're strong enough to come to you."

Like Keras, She waited until I leaned forward hesitantly. She didn't bleed, not like us. Her blood gleamed from inside her skin like a red coal, but it didn't flow out or drip. As soon as I pressed my mouth to the small cut, Her blood filled my mouth. My ears roared with rushing winds and my stomach pitched like the eagle had dropped me off the top of a mountain and let me fall crashing back to earth. She didn't taste like anything specific—it was more of a feeling. Like being swept away. Lost. Only to find myself looking back in the mirror I forgot I was holding.

I opened my eyes but didn't remember closing them. Had I fallen asleep? I couldn't remember. I opened my mouth to ask what had happened, when Keras made a funny sound.

I turned to glare at him, but he wasn't laughing to tease me.

His eyes were soft and glowing with wonder. "Wow. So that's what you wanted in your Blood."

What?

I looked down at my feet.

Hooves.

I had shiny crystal hooves.

Fur. On my legs. *Fur.* Purple and teal and pink and—

I squealed with excitement and it came out like Esperanza's neigh.

:Do I have a horn?: I asked Keras.

:Yes. A long spiral horn that glitters like ice.:

I was so excited I hopped.

Which sent another surge of joy through me. Because when my hooves struck the ground, I sparkled. Glittery lights floated up from the ground like fireflies.

I pranced to the side, sending bright rainbow sparks into the air.

Laughing, even though it came out like a whinny, I raced around Isis, stomping my hooves. Something flashed behind me, and I curved around to look.

At my beautiful, hot pink tail.

I jumped into the air as high as I could and let out a strident neigh. *:Thank you! I love it! I'm a unicorn!:*

"You're most welcome, child." Isis laughed, clapping Her hands. "When you're older, you can have wings too, if you like. I don't think your mother would approve of wings at this age."

Wings. I was going to be a Pegasus unicorn. With pink mane and sparkling hooves and horn…

:This is the best day ever.: I trotted over to Keras and gave him a playful bump with my nose, mindful of my horn. *:I have a new friend, my first Blood, and I'm a unicorn.:*

He smiled, but his eyes echoed with sadness.

My best day… was his worst.

I stepped closer and swung my head around behind his shoulders, so my neck curved around him. *:I'm sorry, Keras.:*

:Don't be sad, my queen. Mama would be very happy that I found a queen like you to serve.:

:My name's Xochitl.:

:Yes, my queen.:

I blew out a snort and stepped back. Mama said Blood could be funny about some things, especially when it came to their queen.

"Let's get you home," Isis said.

I trotted ahead and around them, bouncing with excitement. I couldn't wait to show Mama. *:Keras, shift. Let's race.:*

:I can't…: His eyes widened as his beast flowed out of him. His rhino stared back at me, twice as tall and huge, even if he was young. *:Wow. Thank you, my queen.:*

I wasn't sure what he meant.

"Intention," Isis explained, waiting for us to join her at the tree that should take us home. "You wished him to shift, so he could. You provide the control he needs. He'll never have to struggle to shift, or fear his ability to prevent himself from shifting, again."

I felt so small beside his rhino. I could probably ride him.

As soon as I thought it, I ran at him and jumped as high as I could. My hooves clattered on his hide, but somehow, I managed to scale his muscled shoulder like a goat. Pleased, I walked up and down the length of his broad back, sparkling all over him.

:That tickles.:

Giggling—which came out a whinny—I stomped harder, spinning rainbows all over him.

Isis laughed, a musical sound that flowed around us and made the world dim. As I drifted to sleep, I heard Her words in my head. *:You delight my heart, child of Coatlicue.:*

ABOUT THE AUTHOR

Joely Sue Burkhart has always loved heroes who hide behind a mask, the darker and more dangerous the better. Whether cool, sophisticated billionaire, brutal bloodthirsty assassin, or simply a man tortured by his own needs, they all wear masks to protect themselves. Once they finally give you a peek into the passionate, twisted secrets they're hiding, they always fall hard and fast. Dare to look beneath the mask and find love in the shadows.

Read more from Joely Sue Burkhart and sign up for her newsletter.

ALSO BY JOELY SUE BURKHART

Their Vampire Queen

QUEEN TAKES KNIGHTS

QUEEN TAKES KING

QUEEN TAKES QUEEN

QUEEN TAKES ROOK

QUEEN TAKES CHECKMATE

QUEEN TAKES TRIUNE

Their Vampire Queen novellas

QUEEN TAKES JAGUARS (Mayte)

QUEEN TAKES CAMELOT (Gwen)

Limited Edition Boxed set Captivated

QUEEN TAKES AVALON (Gwen)

Blood & Shadows

THE HORSE MASTER OF SHANHASSON

The Shanhasson Trilogy

THE ROSE OF SHANHASSON

THE ROAD TO SHANHASSON

RETURN TO SHANHASSON

Keldari Fire

SURVIVE MY FIRE

THE FIRE WITHIN

Mythomorphoses

BEAUTIFUL DEATH

The Connaghers

LETTERS TO AN ENGLISH PROFESSOR

DEAR SIR, I'M YOURS

HURT ME SO GOOD

YOURS TO TAKE

NEVER LET YOU DOWN

MINE TO BREAK

THE COMPLETE CONNAGHERS BOXED SET

Billionaires in Bondage

THE BILLIONAIRE SUBMISSIVE

THE BILLIONAIRE'S INK MISTRESS

THE BILLIONAIRE'S CHRISTMAS BARGAIN

Zombie Category Romance

THE ZOMBIE BILLIONAIRE'S VIRGIN WITCH

The Wellspring Chronicles

NIGHTGAZER

A Killer Need

ONE CUT DEEPER

TWO CUTS DARKER

THREE CUTS DEADER

Historical Fantasy Erotica

GOLDEN